MW01200367

THE TOKYO SUITE

Giovana Madalosso

THE TOKYO SUITE

Translated from the Portuguese
by Bruna Dantas Lobato

Europa Editions
27 Union Square West, Suite 302
New York NY 10003
www.europaeditions.com
info@europaeditions.com

This book is a work of fiction. Any references to historical events, real people, or real locales are used fictitiously.

First publication 2025 by Europa Editions

Translation by Bruna Dantas Lobato
Original title: *Suíte Tóquio*

Library of Congress Cataloging in Publication Data is available
ISBN 978-1-60945-980-2

Madalosso, Giovana
The Tokyo Suite

Cover design and illustration by Ginevra Rapisardi

Prepress by Grafica Punto Print – Rome

Printed in Canada

To Carlos and Neuza

“Todo amor é um sacrificio.”
—Arnon Grunberg

THE TOKYO SUITE

1

I'm kidnapping a child. I try to push this thought away, but it keeps coming back as we go down the elevator, say hi to Chico, pass the gates. We do these things every day, go downstairs, say hi to Chico, pass the gates, step on only the black tiles or the white on the sidewalk. But today it's different even if we're not doing anything different, because I know the white army stares at me. Mrs. Fernanda made up this moniker, the white army. And she's not wrong, we really look like an army, especially this early in the morning, when they're all in the piazza in their white nanny uniforms, babies and children in tow, chatting as they push the babies and children on strollers and swings. A world that until yesterday was my world, but that looks at me now with suspicion. Or is it just in my head? Oh Holy Mother, tell me, am I imagining things? I'm not sure, but just in case I pick up the pace, let's go, Corinha, you can step on the white tiles some other time.

I don't cross the piazza as I normally do. Instead, I go around it. Still, the army follow me with their eyes. I run into a nanny from the building next door, and I feel her eying my bag—my sack, really, much bigger than the usual little one, a huge bag I press tight against my body to see if it will shrink. I avoid eye contact and we keep walking, until Cora says: Maju, your hand feels weird; and she lets go of my fingers, maybe to get rid of my sweat. When I look at her, she's already crouched down to pick up a wilted camellia. I never saw a child who loves flowers so much. I think it's nice, a child who loves flowers. This is why

I usually don't rush her, like so many nannies do. I'll let Cora smell an entire garden if she wants, I even carry all her petals in my pocket. Once I forgot them in some pants I put in the washing machine. It was beautiful to see, the flowers inside spinning and dancing. But today we don't have time for that, Chickadee, not today, and I don't even wipe her hands with a wet wipe like I normally do, to make sure they're clean, I just grab those little fingers and don't let go, and feel a pang for the empty of Mandaguaçu, the open of the landscape of Mandaguaçu, because here in São Paulo you can't go one minute without being looked at. Like these cab drivers, watching people's lives to pass the time. I know them all, we only ride with them, Mr. Cacá and Mrs. Fernanda knew them for years. Precisely for this reason, I turn around. I turn around and go up Angélica Avenue. We hop on the bus. Cora thinks it strange. We're not taking a cab, Maju? But she also enjoys the news of it, it's the first time she's ever taken the city bus. She asks to sit at the front, presses her nose on the glass.

The bus station isn't far, and in half an hour we're there. I look around to see if there's anyone I know. Of course not, but I pick up the pace anyway. I tuck Cora into the elevator, the poor thing squeezed between our bags. I've never seen so many people carry so many shopping bags, the crinkling plastic signaling even to the blind that this place is thick with poor people. Thank God the doors open soon, and I leave with my Chickadee. We walk down a platform, and from there we can see many other platforms, people walking side to side, escalators going up and down, signs full of information, lines at the counters, stores with discounts. Cora stops and is still for a moment. I pull her hand, but she doesn't budge. I crouch down to see what's going on. Maju, how are my eyes so small if I see the world so big?

2

My phone is ringing but I decide not to pick up. Yara and I are lying on our backs after a long session of hoka-hoka. I wasn't the one to come up with the name. She told me about it, then showed me the video, female bonobo apes rubbing their genitals against one another. Someone in North Africa decided on this name, which is kind of funny, kind of musical. The voice in the video talks about how female bonobos enjoy having sex with each other more than with male apes. Specialists know this from the way they look their partners in the eye and move a lot more during hoka-hoka. Yara said the voiceover was right. She once saw female bonobos having passionate sex when she was in the Congo Basin. And it was actual *sex*, not just plain mating like other animals, because it was a trade, an exchange of affection. I remember thinking that what defines a verb is not the subject but the object. I've mated with some people; with her I have sex.

It isn't always a fair trade. I've been receiving less than I've been giving. Passion dividends. But this doesn't change the way I look at her, I'm still delighted by even the simplest things, for example the way she holds a joint between her fingers. Even her slurring after smoking weed, which would bother anyone in their right mind, I still like. I like seeing her swimming against the current of productivity, doing the opposite of what I do at work. While I squeeze stories into ten-minute blocks, into eight-episode series, she turns hers into an entire odyssey, as if she really did live in that world she loves so much, ruled by natural cycles instead of by the urgent demands of her smartphone. That and her slightly saggy breasts, like her drooping eyelids, make me take the joint from her fingers and kiss her.

My phone rings again. I glance at it. It's my husband. I put it on silent. I go back to rubbing my genitals against Yara's, while outside hundreds of other primates are driving, with their hairy tails on the driver's seat and opposable thumbs on the horn, causing an uproar in the jungle around us. When we lie back again, I have seven missed calls on my phone.

3

The clock at the bus terminal says it's ten to twelve. I carefully take out the authorization I was keeping in a book so it won't get crumpled and think to myself that I can still go back; until the bus leaves, I'm still the boss of my legs. But then I look down at the paper and remember that I won't have another chance like this, and I go on.

Where are we going? Cora asks. I ignore her question, I think for the first time, as I busy myself with our documents and the boarding pass, rereading the parental authorization. Cacá is the one who wrote it and even got it notarized, so I can accompany the minor Cora de Azevedo Cunha to his parents' house in Rio de Janeiro, a trip that in the end didn't happen but that gave me the idea to use the document, valid for thirty days. And since it's now or never, come on, woman, be brave, the driver barely even looks at the passengers, just wants everyone to get in already, especially since the line outside seems to go on forever, and everyone is so rude. Watch where you're going, lady, I say to a woman who almost run us over. To avoid another stumble, I lift my Chickadee and carry her in my arms. Come here to Maju. She looks up at the bus, amazed at the height of the double-decker. Is this our bus? I tell her yes and give her a kiss, and a fear consumes me, my hands getting sweaty again. Will the driver notice my sweaty hands when I show him the documents? I pray to our Lady of Aparecida and soon he's reading the authorization. He checks my ID and fixes his yellow tie. I don't know why he does that, fix his tie, but he says: enjoy your trip.

I feel my shoulders drop like the suitcase I drop on the seat. I start organizing our things, grabbing what I need so I can put the rest under the bus. Cora pokes my arm, points at the ladder, and says she wants to go up. I crouch down and explain that we can't. Maju got the best seats for us. You see this seat? It turns into a bed. Up there they don't, the seats are small, and don't recline, they're not for a girl like you. But I want to go up there, she repeats, and seeing that I don't move, that we'll stay right here, she pouts and starts to cry. I know Cora, she is no spoiled child, so if she's crying like this it's because she really cares. I think about taking her, but maybe then it will be even worse, she'll want to stay there in the regular seats. I don't move. Her crying gets worse and my anxiety too, because of course everyone's staring at us, exactly what I don't want, to draw attention to us. I can already picture it in the news: I remember them because the little girl was crying, the little girl didn't want to go with her. To prevent this and to get Cora to calm down, I put her on my lap, run my hand over her hair, but instead of stopping, she cries harder, her mouth split almost in half. The couple sitting in front of us look annoyed, imagining a hell of a trip, and I keep repeating: it's okay, Corinha, how about I let you sit at the window. But she doesn't care and insists: I want to go up there, and hearing the sound of her voice makes it even more painful, because now her cries sound more hurt. How I miss the pacifier days. We must all carry pacifiers in our pockets forever—no one will need cigarettes or tranquilizers or nail biting anymore. Now she will suck hers and I mine, the other passengers will suck theirs, everyone will feel just peachy. This reminds me of something else. Her baby, of course. The sheep, which I now take out of my bag and give to Cora. I put it in her hand, and to my surprise it only makes things worse. Looking at her friend, she kicks and screams. Bibi and I want to go up there. Usually, I let her cry until she sleeps. It's the right thing so she can learn, but today it's not possible. I rummage through my bag, and fish out a packet of salt and one of pepper, four toothpicks, and, finally, a sugar packet. I wish Neide was here to see what I'm doing. She always says hoarding these is a poor person's habit, something for people with nothing else to own. Look, Neide, and tell me it's not useful, I think while I pour a cup of water and dump in the sugar. I give it to Cora, but since I know her all too well, I say: drink this, Chickadee, but leave some for Bibi. She's very careful, so she stops crying a little as she pays attention to the bit of water she'll save for the sheep. I feel my breathing slow down with hers. I congratulate Cora and Bibi for drinking it all and quickly make the cup disappear with the water that can prove the sheep's tummy doesn't really exist. Then I move Cora to her seat, put a pillow behind her head, and spread the blanket over her legs. She looks out the window. Where are we going, Maju? I can't tell her the name of the town, not in front of the other passengers, and she won't care either, so I tell her what she wants to hear: to a beautiful place. A place full of little animals that work at night.

4

I get into the elevator and check the time, 9:15 P.M. Then I look at myself in the mirror and do what my daughter would do: I press the button to the third floor, and all the ones before it. I can't go into our house looking so self-satisfied. My face flushed, my eyebrows all over the place, my hair disheveled. I have fine hair, all tangled up now thanks to the hoka-hoka. While the elevator is on the first floor, I toss the knotted mess behind my head and tie it up with an elastic band, then smooth my eyebrows, and rehearse a facial expression that makes me look like I had a normal day.

As I walk through the door, I quickly realize I could have come in with a hickey on my forehead and it wouldn't have mattered. Cacá is sitting on the armchair, leaning forward, his hands holding his head, heavy like a cast-iron ball. He says he's been trying to reach Maju since the first time he called me, at 7 P.M., but she hasn't answered. He's already called the neighbor and Cora's best friend, but no sign of her or the nanny. I ask if he's tried my mother. She sometimes stops by to see her granddaughter and takes her out somewhere. He says he has, but her phone was off or out of range. Then a lightbulb goes off in my head. My mother has a farm near Avaré, a place so remote phones only work if you stand between this rock and that jackfruit tree—so we renamed it the Hard Rock Cafe. Perhaps she took Cora to the farm. After all she's done this on several holidays and weekends, picking up both Cora and the nanny after school. I call for our maid, Cida, who tells us that Maju and Cora left early in the morning carrying a huge bag and a Tupperware. We guess they went to the club, had lunch over there, as they often do, and got on the road with my mother after school. In a flash, Cacá runs to Cora's bedroom and comes back saying that Bibi is gone too. It takes me a moment to realize who Bibi is. At first I think it might be a friend of my mother's, one of those chronically drunk and nostalgic old ladies who never leave the house. But then I remember it's the stuffed sheep and I smile at Cacá. The fact that they took Cora's baby is more evidence that they expect to sleep away from home. Of course my mother should have asked us first. Or at least warned us. But in truth I don't expect much from her, she's never been the most considerate. One time she even came into our house and took a TV without asking, alleging that hers was broken and she couldn't go without her soaps. Maju, on the other hand, is so considerate it gets exhausting. She sends me pictures and videos of Cora all day long—as if I've never seen her eating an apple or smelling a flower—so it's unusual that she hasn't so much as texted, not a single picture of Cora on the road. She must have run out of battery or something. We decide to keep calling my mother and just in case we also call some of Cora's friends.

First, I need a break. From the problems at home, the problems at work, the passion that's burning my skin. I make myself a drink. With the glass in one hand and the phone in the other, I look for the numbers of the other school moms, only to remember I left the group. Cacá's contacts are more up-to-date, so I let him make the calls.

Already a little tipsy, lying on the living room rug, I listen to my husband talk to women I've never heard of, about children I've never heard of, about events I had no idea happened, like a lice outbreak at the school. While he talks to the mom of a kid named Bebel, I think about how I've come to be a tourist in my own house, floating on a rug with a cocktail in hand, replying to thumbs-up emojis with tongue emojis.

5

Finally, the road. And not the slums that surround the city like vultures around carrion. The proper road, that open I love so much, just a skinny cow here and there, the fields and little houses, the quiet of the houses, the earth already changing colors from brown to purple, from purple to red. I show Corinha the landscape, but she is busy looking at the snacks we got on the bus. Cracker nuts and cookies, which we sure won't eat. Mrs. Fernanda says that water and salt bind the bowels. I explain to Cora that this is junk, we'll eat something way better. I grab our packed lunch, the pasta salad with tomato and zucchini that she loves. The woman in front of us smells the food and tells the man next to her, honey, if they keep this up, we'll have to move. I think that's a great idea, I don't want anyone making faces at me, or commenting on our food, and especially listening to our conversations, so I say very loud: now Maju will get the chicken! Even though there is no chicken. The woman scoffs and says: Come on, there's room upstairs. The two of them go with their bags. Thank God, because now I can finally talk with my Chickadee.

While I tear the package of the plastic fork, I tell Cora we're going to a town called Presidente Prudente, really far away, past what she thinks is the countryside. Then I sit quiet, chewing, thinking we're going to arrive at six thirty and that right about that time people will start noticing us gone, but that's fine, because we'll be in a cab by then, on our way to Ponta Porã, where we'll cross the border on foot all the way to Pedro Juan Caballero, in Paraguay, where I think I can get Cora a new ID. When I was a teenager in the north of Paraná, the grandson of one of my grandmother's friends smuggled cars across the border, and when things got rough, he traveled to Pedro Juan to get himself a new identity. I remember he always came back with imported sneakers, new hair and a new name. Who knew that God would put me on the same path as Antônio who was Serginho who was Pablo who was Diego? And since it was God who put me here on this path, I won't feel bad, I'll fulfill my purpose. I tell Cora let's do something crazy, something very fun, change her name. I ask her what name she wants from now on. Moana, she says. I say it can't be that one, too princess-y, too Disney. How about something normal, like Manuela, Carolina, Brígida, like my grandmother? She doesn't answer, too concentrated on balancing the spaghetti on her fork, so I'll have to get back to it later, choose a name already and get Cora out of our minds. I think it will be okay because I was around the same age when my mother died and I don't remember much from that time, only a charm hanging on her neck, a golden cross that twirled when I sat on her lap.

I wipe Cora's mouth with a napkin I got at Casa do Pão, then peel a tangerine. I pinch out the seeds and give her the segments, while I tell her that from Presidente Prudente we're going to travel a bit longer until we get to our final destination, Mandaguaçu, where Maju was born. And then she'll see what beautiful lives we'll have. We'll wake up in nature and ride tractors, pick leaves off mulberry trees, tons and tons of them, because the silkworms don't eat anything else. In the day, we'll feed the little creatures. You have to see how much they eat. They stay inside their cocoon just chewing day and night. At first they're not too much trouble because they're so small, but when they're ready for their next life, they eat for six days straight, their mouths already large, tongues grinding and grinding the leaves, and they sound like rain hitting the ground. They eat so much we have to wake up in the middle of the night to add more leaves, and then the most beautiful part starts, God's part, when out of the silkworm's mouth comes thread. You have to see it, Chickadee, the silk threads coming out their mouths. We take the silkworms to the woods, to little crates where they weave their own cocoons, their own little houses. It's the most beautiful thing.

Are these worms real, Maju? I say they sure are, but no need to be scared, they're very nice. When Maju was a kid she liked to grab them by the handful like this, and I show her the imaginary worms in my fingers. Then you know what they become? Butterflies! I say, to see if she gets excited, but she says she's still scared. I run my fingers through her hair, which are also threads woven by nature, and I change the subject to calm her down. I tell her we'll also take care of other things at the farm, feed chickens, rabbits, piglets. Real rabbits? I say yes and she claps. I feel good, I feel so good, I tell her about all the swimming she'll do at the lake, about the little garden we'll grow inside a wheelbarrow, about the tire swing we'll hang from a plum tree, about the dog she'll finally have. Then I remember the other issue. The name, Chickadee, what name do you want? She thinks for a moment and says: Nina, maybe because she has a friend called Nina. I say: not Nina, as I think about rich people's habit of giving kids short names: Teo, Lia, Noa, Lara, Olga, Max, Oto, even Oto these people will name a kid, I don't understand why they're so stingy with their letters. If letters are free, why not use them, have names that can fill up your mouth. I suggest one from the book I'm reading, Rosalind. Isn't it pretty, Chickadee? She says it isn't, it's ugly, and prefers Elsa like the princess in *Frozen*. I say it can't be Elsa, it's a woman's name, people will think she's a grown woman and here comes a tiny little girl with her Bibi under one arm. It doesn't work. Maju is only saying this because she wants what's best for you. Cora thinks for a moment and says: Ana, like the other princess in *Frozen*. Ana is short, but it's not that bad, and I need to respect her choices. All right, Chickadee, your name is Ana now.

6

It was humiliating, getting hit by a two-year-old. It happened on a flight from Rio de Janeiro to São Paulo. We were coming back from a weekend at Cacá's parents. Normally, Cacá would have gone home with us, but this time he had to stay in Rio for a minor procedure, and since he wanted to rest in his mother's care, he stayed behind, while I flew back with our daughter. We boarded the plane, sat down, and I placed Cora in the seat next to me. When I tried to buckle her seatbelt, she grabbed my hand. I wasn't surprised, she'd always hated seatbelts, and would sometimes make a fuss about getting in the car. But on the plane, it was particularly bad. She snatched the buckle from my hand and started crying and kicking with a strength that I find impressive to this day, as if inside that baby were a grown adult pushing to come out. I tried everything, but with all her kicking and screaming, I couldn't manage to secure her seatbelt. When it finally clicked into place over her diaper and I thought it was all over, to my astonishment, she slapped me across the face. A loud slap, right out of a soap opera, despite the size of her hand. I had no reaction. And realizing the power in her gesture—the ability to make me freeze—she slapped me again, and would have continued hadn't I grabbed her hand in time, firmly, taken by my own fit of anger. Every mother at some point has wished for their kid to disappear. To die for a few seconds.

Because of the endless crying, all of row 14 was staring at me. And so were row 13 and 15. Only then did I notice the flight attendant had been standing next to us for a while, watching the scene, as she checked that every passenger's seatbelt was fastened before the plane took off. And now ours were, they finally were. As the plane started to move, I told the flight attendant, we're fine. I held Cora's hands to keep her from striking again but I gripped her too tightly, which upset her and made her scream even louder. As soon as the plane was steady and I let go of her, she struck me in the face again. It wasn't an issue between mother and daughter anymore, but a spectacle for an audience of passengers. Some were lucky (or unlucky) enough to witness the whole drama, while others could only hear it, with the nosiest types trying to catch a glimpse of what was happening over at fiery 14F. That was when, without even realizing, I took the stage. I got up and started to walk with her up and down the aisle to try and calm her, rocking her and singing some desperate verses of "Alecrim dourado," all while the passengers stared and listened. Suddenly there came a little hand and slapped me one more time. I remember the expression on people's faces at that moment, staring at me, divided into two groups: the ones who looked at me with pity and the ones who looked at me with contempt, asking themselves: how can a mother be so powerless? Yes, I wondered that too. I didn't know what to do, I couldn't hit my daughter and disciplining her was proving to be difficult. I quickly walked to the bathroom and locked the door. I put Cora on the ground and started to cry. Me standing, her sitting down, both of us crying for what felt like such a long time I relived every version of me I'd ever been. We only got back to our seats when the flight attendant announced the plane would soon be landing, and luckily Cora was so exhausted by then I easily buckled her up.

After we landed, I kept my head down all the way from when I grabbed our bags to when we walked out of the airport. Only as I got into the cab did I finally feel free of the embarrassment, having left behind anyone who might have witnessed my humiliation. I rolled down the window, hoping for the wind to take what I was feeling with it. I stayed like that, with my face to the street, while Cora slept in my arms.

We got home, I tucked her in bed, and headed to my bedroom. Although I was exhausted, I couldn't sleep. I kept thinking about where my daughter's anger towards me had come from. Anger for having been vanquished—perhaps the same anger I felt for having been vanquished in my role as a mother. Cora felt that. Even if we don't know everything, we always know everything. She must have sensed my anxiety about the decision I had to make, which would also affect her. I had just received an offer from the TV channel I worked for to leave my role as content director and become an executive producer, the highest-ranking position in the company in Brazil. At first I'd refused, because if I accepted I'd have to report to Los Angeles, working on both time zones, and would be left with no time for my daughter. But of course I wasn't at peace with my decision. I wanted that position and I realized that being a frustrated mother wasn't a great plan, because I'd end up passing all my bitterness down to my daughter. Better to spend less time together—as the childrearing gurus would put it—and make every second count.

It wasn't midnight yet, so I decided to call my husband to say I'd changed my mind and would accept the offer. He didn't question it, as I was the one who supported us; it was my decision to make. After we hung up, I slept very lightly, to the point I heard Maju come in and hang something on the hallway coat rack. I put on a robe and went to her. I took her to the kitchen for a cup of coffee. I needed to be very convincing. In a way, it all depended on her. I used the experience I'd gained hiring the people on my team: offer a reasonable sum then increase it immediately, making it seem as though you've ended up giving more than originally planned, that the offer is so extraordinary it can't be refused. I did this with Maju, but even so she was apprehensive, and with good reason. I remember that in that moment I felt kind of satanic, smoking my cigarette with my hair disheveled and my red robe, selling her a future full of money and riches, a future that maybe—especially as I had yet to accept the offer—might never come, though maybe it would, how could I know? If only Maju were smarter and had just asked me for more money. She couldn't have known, but in that moment I would have given her everything: how much for you to stay here all the time, six times the minimum wage plus the gold ring on my finger? Consider it done, I'll sign you on a video editor's salary, because you're much more valuable to me than a video editor. But Maju was too humble and innocent to dream beyond what God or her boss had offered her. So after she accepted, I felt sorry. To make it up to her, I turned the tiny maid's room into a bright and modern space full of amenities like a TV and a mini-fridge, a room that could well be a suite in a Japanese hotel. For this reason, and also so I could feel less colonial in my role as her boss, I named the room Tokyo Suite.

A month later, a new salary went into her account and a new one into mine. I looked at the numbers not knowing what to do. I thought of taking a trip, but it wasn't the right time for a vacation. I thought of buying jewelry, but I already had plenty and I wasn't one carat happier for it. Talking to a friend, I got the idea of buying art. I went to a gallery that had an Adriana Varejão painting. Small but powerful: a sauna of white tiles stained with blood. I bought my gift and hung it in the living room, arguing with Cacá that though the painting had cost a fortune, it wasn't an extravagance but an investment, property we'd leave for our daughter.

7

Cora falls asleep. I settle in my seat and look out the window. Everything moves so fast out there. I feel it's my life passing by, twenty-seven years of São Paulo disappear in a blur. How can so much change in so little time? I bring Cora with me, a wad of cash, and five dentures. The rest is memories, it's all we have, but in truth that's nothing. Memory is a stillborn child. Already decomposing. How hard I fight for Lauro to never decompose. Can I keep his face from disappearing by thinking about him every day? Because the pictures and videos I deleted long ago, in a moment of anger after what he did to me, and all I have now are the pictures and videos my mind wants to keep, and I keep wondering how our brain decides, because some things disappear and others remain so whole, all that's missing is a play button. Like our beginning. I was working at Mrs. Tarsila's, washing her sidewalk every single day. I mean, Monday through Friday. They didn't have kids, she and Mr. Ronaldo, but her quirks kept me really busy, like pressure-washing her sidewalk, which I must hose and mop every day, rain or shine. The rain in São Paulo only gets it dirtier not cleaner, Mrs. Tarsila said, and there I went to re-wash the just-washed tiles, to polish what was already polished, preparing the sidewalk for I don't know who to lick, not Mrs. Tarsila for sure, since she herself never left the house. The whole day she spent reading and eating chocolates, that big ass on the couch, smelling like baby powder, because she loved to put it on the folds of her skin to avoid rashes. She never even got up to answer the phone. She was so proud of never having washed a single glass in her life. And I don't doubt it. I could only go to sleep when she and Mr. Ronaldo went to bed, when there wasn't any chance of a cream cheese knife popping up in the sink, at around ten, eleven at night. When they had friends over for dinner, usually on Fridays, I had to stay until the middle of the night to clean everything. Those times, they paid for a cab to get home alright, and that's how I met Lauro. I gave no attention to his face at first because I was used to not look at men. At that point, I'd only had one man in my life, a janitor at one of the many places where I'd worked, on Franca Avenue, and it was so sad with this janitor, because I was a silly seventeen-year-old girl. He offered to help me with my grocery bags and I thought he wanted to date me. He opened the elevator door for me and I thought he wanted to marry me. Until the day he called me up to his little room on the top floor and I understood full well what he wanted. He covered my mouth with a cloth that smelled of metal polish and put me on all fours on his twin bed, the blood staining the flowers on the sheets and he going on: this bitch is a virgin, this bitch is a virgin, the smell of Brasso burning my nostrils. Since that day I always cry when I polish silver. Everyone knows me for polishing my boss's trays with a mix of Brasso and tears. Of course I never wanted anything to do with men anymore. So I didn't see Lauro. That Friday I was in the back seat of the cab, minding my own business, until he started to change the radio stations. He stopped at a song and asked: you like this one? I'm not one to listen to music for fun, I don't have time for that stuff, so I just said: hmm, that's all. But a few minutes later, during the ads, he changed stations again and asked: and what about this one, do you like it? This time I knew the song. It was "Chico Mineiro," it played on the radio all the time when I was a girl in the countryside in Paraná. I said I liked it. He said he did too and turned up the volume. Tonico & Tinoco sang the way we do in Mandaguaçú. Imremember, lasttaim, malove. I felt my grandmother by my side and my eyes filled with tears. Lauro saw it in the rearview mirror and smiled at me. He didn't say anything else that day. I paid the ride, got my change, but noticed he waited for me to get in the rusty gates to my house before he left.

Two weeks later, Mr. Ronaldo called the cab company and there was Lauro again. The same thing happened but it was a little different, the way life always is, more of the same but different. Same address? he asked and I nodded. Then he turned on the radio. You like this one? And so we went the whole way, he looking for songs and asking me if I liked whatever was playing, and turning up the volume when I said yes. When we arrived, the same thing, he waited for my gate to creak open then drove away. It went on like this for weeks, months. Of course it didn't always happen that I rode with him. The first driver in line came, but after a while Lauro was coming more and more. He saw that Mr. Ronaldo always called on Fridays at around one in the morning, and kept watch, so he was always the first in line waiting for the phone to ring. I made some changes too. I started to wear some clothes I found at a shop near the station, all very tight, like they've run out of fabric, some blouses I then got rid of because they weren't really me, but it was nice to wear them at the time. And lipstick, for the first time I wore lipstick, a pink shade I remember the name to this day, Sweet Poison.

I already knew more than twenty songs he liked and still I had no clue his name was Lauro, because the bastard was so shy, even more than me, who was already slow as a turtle. Or better yet, an ostrich, with my head stuck in the window. But the silence wasn't bad. As I soon understood, Lauro was a man of few words. And I was quiet too, the noise all inside my head. So it was good, our silence was a pretty long conversation for people like us who aren't naturally chatty. One day it was Carnaval and Mrs. Tarsila decided to throw a masquerade ball, and I had no idea that so late on a Monday he'd be the one to pick me up. But he showed up. And I wasn't even dressed up, no lipstick or even a shower, all sweaty from vacuuming the confetti off the rug. I remember I untied my hair quickly before I got into the taxi, hoping the mop would adorn my face and get his attention away from my ears. No need to tell him where we were going, he knew, like I already knew what we'd do on the way, that we'd listen to music. I just didn't know which songs I wanted yet, and I liked that too, not knowing. But this night was different in every way because it was Carnaval.

Mrs. Tarsila lived in Alto de Pinheiros. To get to my house we needed to cross Vila Madalena, full of bars and people out on the streets. So of course by the time we got to Fradique we had to stop at a crossroads for the parade, people falling over drunk but still strong on the drums and the bugle, a woman with her breasts hanging out and holding a flag. I remember it well because our car was the first to stop for the herd to go by, the line of cars growing behind us. Any driver would hate this situation, but Lauro was Lauro, never lost his temper over the small stuff, he watched the people, some boys in bras, a girl dressed as an odalisque, another as a nun. Suddenly Lauro did something he'd never done, he turned off the radio. I thought it was strange, what's the matter with him? But then I started hearing it. *If you're being honest, ohhh Aurora*. Do you like that one? I nodded. Good that you like it, because I can't change this one, he said, and we laughed, and kept looking ahead, at the flock moving forward. After a while, without turning around, he started to talk. He said he was born in a village called Picinguaba, on the São Paulo coast, a fisherman's son. When he was little he stayed with his mother. In the morning they wove baskets and in the afternoon they peeled and deveined shrimp, but when he was almost ten, he started to go on the raft with his father and loved not having to tear off prawns' intestines with a toothpick. The sea had a calm he liked, though it also had the net, the fish down there fighting to survive. Of course no fisherman worth his salt thinks about that, about the fish's pain before death. But he was a child and thought about this stuff, or he was just weak and thought about it, anyway the point is that one day they caught a twelve-kilo red snapper, a fish with a huge red tail and a golden body, a fish that looked like it was painted by God, and he hated seeing that beautiful thing flailing and hitting the hull. He held the fish in his arms like a baby and rocked it, like his mother did with his little brother, singing and whispering: it's all right, it's all right . . . until the fish moved less and less and died in his arms. Or almost died, because a moment before that happened, Lauro's father hit him with so much anger he broke his nose, the boat and the fish all covered in blood. You see it's a bit crooked on this side? Lauro asked me, tilting his head, while the parade still went by. I never noticed, I said. And it was true, because I'd only ever seen his nose from one side, the side I could see from the back. When I was fourteen, I left home, came to São Paulo all by myself, he said. Then he was quiet, again looking ahead. I wanted to pat him on the shoulder, but of course I couldn't do that, I might give the wrong impression if I touched a man like that. So I decided to do something else instead, to tell him something about myself, which wasn't easy because, our Lady of Aparecida, I'm so shy my heart races when I so much as think of speaking, but I tried really hard and told him I was raised by my grandmother, always just the two of us, and that when she knew her time was close, she quickly found a home for me to work in São Paulo, because she wanted me to go to college, work during the day and study at night. That was why I moved here, because she told me, she put the address in my hand, Artur de Azevedo 143, and I came with it crumpled in my fingers, crying from Mandaguaçu all the way here. When I arrived, I found out the boss had a baby and that I needed to take care of him at night too, which wasn't all bad because I love babies, but for years I felt bad I didn't honor my grandma Brígida's wish and became a teacher. And did you want to be a teacher? Lauro asked. I said no, and we laughed, and we heard the honks, the parade was almost gone so we could go ahead.

We went all the way to my house without talking, as usual, just listening to the radio. When we got there, he didn't stop in the middle of the street but parked in a little spot right in front of my gate. I handed him the money for the ride but he didn't want it, he pushed it away, got out of the car and opened the door for me. Then he walked to the gate with me and asked: can I? I was scared, a strange feeling, the smell of Brasso in my head or in my nose, I don't even know. But then Lauro held my purse while I looked for my keys and I felt calm. Maybe *calm* isn't the right word, my hands were sweaty, that real man coming into my house, and I was worried if the house looked clean. I hid a dirty cloth I'd left on the sink very quickly, and said, don't mind the mess, but he didn't even look, he went straight to the stereo next to the TV, a small one I'd got from Mrs. Tarsila but had never even turned on. He grabbed one of the LPs I also got from her and said, can I put on some Elton John? He was careful and took the record from the sleeve, placed the needle on it. I didn't know that song, though now I know it well, as I've listened to it again and again many times since, "Blue Eyes." And when I didn't expect it, that big man standing next to me raised a hand and asked me to dance. I moved close to him, my nose touching his beard, which smelled so nice my face went red. I thought: don't be so stupid, woman, and just thinking I was stupid made my face go even redder. Before Lauro noticed, I said: let me grab something and I'll be right back. I looked inside my purse for the mask someone abandoned at the party, a purple face with a white tear, a sad but pretty face. Mrs. Tarsila said it must be Venetian, and that yes, I may keep it. I thought it would look nice if I hung it on the wall, never imagined wearing it on my face that same night. But suddenly there I was with it on, seeing Lauro through the slits for the eyes, his hand in the air waiting for me again. I danced to "Blue Eyes," until he grabbed me in his arms and laid me on the couch, and very slowly took off my blouse, blowing away the confetti on my sweaty chest, one by one.

After that night, Lauro started to pick me up at work every Friday night and staying longer and longer, until Saturday and soon all weekend, until one day he brought all his stuff and then some. He brought his 43-inch TV, put his shoes next to mine, his Bible next to my books. I stayed at Mrs. Tarsila's Monday through Thursday, so when he picked me up on Fridays we missed each other so much we needed the whole night together to recover. We woke up late on Saturday, always the last ones to arrive at the farmers market. He loved choosing what to make for lunch. He liked fish, I think it reminded him of his mom. He taught me how to skin the fillet in a way I'd never seen. The two of us faced the sink, each one with a knife cleaning the fish, sometimes our elbows touched and we giggled. Then he started to cook and drink beer, a dish towel always hanging on his shoulder, an LP playing, it was certain at one point he'd ask me to dance. He called me Nhazinha, because he said I was a farm girl, and he did so much for me. One day he showed up with a dog. Now that I'm always at home you can have a dog, he said, and I called that pretty girl Bionic. I don't even think I knew what the word meant, but I thought it was funny, Bionic! I yelled out as I threw my shoe for her to catch. Just around that time, Mrs. Tarsila and Mr. Ronaldo moved to Guarujá and I had to look for another job. I ended up at Mrs. Fernanda's, and at first I was glad that I got to work the same number of hours I worked at Mrs. Tarsila's, but with more money and only to take care of a child, Corinha, who was just a baby at the time. But one day, I don't know what got into Mrs. Fernanda, I arrived early a Monday morning and she was drinking coffee looking like she got no sleep, her red robe crumpled, her hair all over the place. She said she had an offer, asked if I wanted more money, not two times the minimum wage, three times so I'd stay there all the time, only take every other Sunday off. I said thank you for the offer, it's a sin to look down on a good thing, but I said I couldn't, me and Lauro want to have a baby, going home only twice a month wouldn't work. At the time she still smoked. I remember she lit a cigarette, tapped off the ashes on the first saucer she saw, said that she really liked me, and for that reason she's going to make me another offer, four times the minimum wage plus healthcare. Don't I want a child? Imagine how wonderful giving birth in a private hospital. But for that I needed to get pregnant first, Mrs. Fernanda. Then she asked me if I had a regular cycle. I said like clockwork. So she suggested I have every other Sunday off, and whenever I ovulate. I just had to keep track on a calendar and I could go sleep at home. I had right to one conjugal visit per month.

At the time that phrase bothered me, conjugal visit, it sounded more like I was a prisoner. But soon Mrs. Fernanda started to talk about the money, that on top of it she'd make sure we had all the right paperwork, that I could finance a house, put my child in a private school, that kind of thing. I said I need to talk to my husband. I went to the little laundry room and called him. Lauro said he preferred me to say no, but since he couldn't afford what Mrs. Fernanda is offering me, to do what my heart told me. I went to the window in the laundry room and looked out for a moment, remembering all the women I'd seen in line at the employment agency, thinking of the time when I was one of them, and all the bosses who said during the interviews that they loved me and would call me soon but never did. I also thought of what grandma Brígida would think of me refusing such money, a teacher's salary. So I told Mrs. Fernanda that alright, I accept.

On the day of the conjugal visit, Lauro canceled whatever ride he had to pick me up. We drove home while we listened to music, me in the passenger seat, next to him, one putting a hand on the other's leg, he carrying me to bed in his arms, and it was good like this for a few months. Some days I was tired and Lauro was too, or something happened that bothered one of us. We were no kids, both already middle-aged, sometimes there was nothing to get him in the mood, but even so we cuddled in bed. Until at one point even love was missing, because when I got home on Sundays it was already so late, there was no farmers market or fish to skin together anymore. We didn't have a whole day for Lauro to get excited over beer and ask me to dance, and so each time we grew a little more distant, like the kitchen table where we ate our dinner was growing between us, meters and meters of table between us, until we barely heard each other anymore, and we didn't understand each other like we used to. All this I know now, but at the time I didn't know what was happening, our love was like that fruit that rots from the inside and no one can see it. All I knew was that slowly Lauro stopped picking me up at Mrs. Fernanda's, or making us dinner, or hugging me while I slept until one day I got home for one of the conjugal visits and felt a shooting pain in my chest because Bionic didn't run to the door to see me, and that had never happened before.

I opened the door already knowing what I would find, or what I wouldn't, because he wasn't there. The hammock was missing from the corner of the living room, the basket his mother made, his toolbox, the Bible from the bookcase, the clothes from the closet, and the dog, he had taken the dog. I screamed like a pig before slaughter. How could he leave before he even talked to me? I curled up on the bedroom floor and cried, cried in a way I hadn't cried since my grandma's death, feeling abandoned all over again, by Lauro and by my dog and by the child I hadn't even had. The more I thought about this, the more it hurt, because I didn't even blame that bastard, he left the same way he came, without a single word, that was how he was, and he took Bionic because he knew I couldn't take care of her, he wanted to spare me. Thinking of that and also of the 43-inch TV he left for me, I cried more, out of anger and love, out of love and anger.

I tried calling Lauro several times, I left so many messages, but he never picked up or returned my calls, which made me believe maybe he met someone else and didn't want to tell me. I was so upset that for months I cried at work, to the point Mrs. Fernanda, who was never even home, started noticing and asked me what was wrong. No way I could tell her the truth, because if she knew that Lauro was gone, bye bye Sundays off, no more conjugal visits, she'd make me stay in the Tokyo Suite forever. And of course I didn't want that. We need a home to go back to sometime, a place where we can sit on the couch, choose what we want to eat, leave a dirty glass in the sink. I told Mrs. Fernanda I was sad but didn't know why. She said: that's depression, you can't bring this kind of sadness to Cora, I'll take you to my psychiatrist. I was thankful, God knows how much something like that costs, but of course I didn't accept it, a pill couldn't fix my problem. I told her not to worry because I'm going to stop crying. A few days later I discovered something interesting: we can save tears the way we save coins. I saved a whole two weeks' worth of tears, and opened the safe on my Sundays off. The key was the Elton John album. I lay down in the living room with the curtains drawn, put on "Blue Eyes," and sobbed so loud I woke up the neighbors.

8

I was on a show, standing on an orange and blue stage with four other contestants, surrounded by a live audience. The host challenged us to find our husbands' skull in the pile in front of us. Whoever found it first won. The pile was massive, towering over us, a mountain of bones stacked on bones, like the clean remains of a gruesome ritual. The host announced the start of the competition. We lunged at the pile. I snatched a skull and held it in the air in a Hamlet pose, but quickly let it go: it was too big to be Cacá's. I grabbed another, then another, but they all looked the same. Dental arches, when closed shut, look like a frozen smile, a curious embrace between humor and death. But none of those macabre grins resembled the one I was looking for. I went on rummaging through that cemetery, a clattering of bones, the audience cheering, until a contestant finally found hers. It's Roberto's, she screamed, dashing in her high heels to place the tiny skull on a pedestal. A light turned on and announced her victory. Congratulations, the host yelled. Yet the challenge must continue. I picked up the search with the other women, until one of them screamed: Ernesto. And another: Flávio. And another: Reinaldo, and I was left alone with the pile, now all scattered, the skulls rolling across the stage as I crawled in search of my husband's head. Does he have all four of his wisdom teeth? asked a voice coming from the audience, and I realized I didn't know. Before I could answer, I heard laughter so intense yet so contained it sounded like a claque. Maybe it was a claque. I grabbed a random skull and announced: it's him. Then I ran to the last pedestal, put the skull on it, and felt the confetti rain down on me. There was no one left on the stage or in the audience.

At the time, I didn't understand this dream. Maybe because our subconscious is always ahead and, like all visionaries, it seems delirious or incomprehensible to anyone still in the fog of the present. Only later did I start to grasp something, the distance between me and Cacá. Not that our marriage was bad. But it was a marriage, with the subtle deadly force of most marriages. And with such an absence of conflict that no matter what happened beneath the surface, everything always seemed fine.

I think that's what drew me in at first, how everything always seemed fine. We loved going out to drink and dance, always the last ones to leave the dance floor; we'd talk all the way home, no matter the time. What most people would have considered as flaws weren't flaws to me. Like how he never stuck with a job. He studied to be an architect, but then changed his mind. He tried model making for a while, but that didn't last either. Later he found other jobs, like the terrariums, the trendy mini gardens that seemed promising for a while. He spent his days bent over the glass globes with his tweezers in hand, gluing little houses, mushrooms, and tiny men next to the cacti and succulents, which, on that scale, looked as monumental as sequoias. I remember how long it took to place a balloon in the hand of a woman the size of my thumb. It was complicated, because the object needed to float—what's the point of a balloon stuck to the ground—and hardening that string was a hell that Cacá took on on his knees, waiting for the glue on the string to dry in the sun. Of course the terrariums weren't worth the time he spent on them, but they kept him at home, taking care of the things I couldn't take care of myself. Which, deep down, was also his plan. Cacá liked domestic life; he was born to care for things, whatever they were. The cacti, our rose bushes, Cora, my mother, our friends, our apartment renovation, our parties, our weekday dinners. Even if I wanted to, I couldn't manage everything he did, at least not with that lightness, which I really admired. I understood that just as I needed to go somewhere far away to thrive, he needed to focus on the little things.

Of course the sex wasn't keeping our neighbors up. Especially after Cora was born. It happens to every mother. How can you feel lust when you've just stopped being your own person? Because for a time that might be days, months, or years, the mother is doubled, connected to the child they birthed by a second, invisible cord. During that time, we only had sex a few times. Later we established an amount acceptable for life in society. It wasn't a perfect world, but, as I learned from Cacá, there are no perfect worlds, not even in terrariums, where hearts are made of putty. So things were fine by me. I would work, he would take care of the home, we'd go out dancing once a week, travel twice a year, and joined the local club. That is, I was already set to die. But then life came to find me again.

It happened during the first production meeting for *The Good Wilderness*, a TV series I deeply believed in, because it challenged the common belief that there are good and bad animals, offering a more comprehensive understanding of top predators. To achieve this, I had to leave behind the traditional observational documentary style, and give alligators, otters, snakes, jaguars, and others drama worthy of any lead character, featuring moments of heroism, villainy, compassion, and even romance. This series was also unique because nine out of ten episodes would be shot in Brazil on a very low production budget, then marketed abroad in dollars. For all these reasons, on that Tuesday I headed with my team to a meeting at the production company in a hip warehouse on the West Side of São Paulo.

All in all, there were about fifteen people sitting around that long oval table. I didn't know her, and she didn't know me either, and we weren't even introduced on that first day, because as the meeting was about to start, a hummingbird appeared. It came into the room through the door that opened onto the garden. Once it was in, it couldn't leave. It flew to the top of the glass wall and flapped its wings, trying to get back to the garden through the transparent obstacle. I must admit, had I been the only one there, the hummingbird would have died. I didn't know anything about birds and their needs. In fact, I didn't know anything about animals in general. Until my promotion, I'd only ever worked on art and travel documentaries. Only later was I put in charge of everything the channel produced in Brazil, including the nature shows. That was why I thought nothing needed to be done about the bird. Then a young woman in jeans and a t-shirt dragged a table against the glass wall. It's using too much energy, she said, already climbing up the chair and then the table. If it goes too long without eating, it'll die. I think someone said: get down, you'll fall, but she already had her hands cupped, catching the hummingbird and quickly stepping down from the chair on firm ground. To my surprise, she came to me. Maybe because I was near the door to the garden. Maybe because of reasons not even our documentaries could explain. She addressed me directly, showing off the hummingbird, lying it on its back in her hands. She told me to pay attention to its eyes. I did, they were tiny, entirely black, shiny circles darting from side to side. It's trying to figure out where it is, she told me. Once it does, it'll fly away. She went out in the garden, waited for the bird to gather its bearings and leave her hand. Then she came back and took her seat. It took a while for someone to explain to me who she was, and in those few minutes, even without knowing of her importance or how interesting she was, I was already drawn to her. Not physically, I'd never felt attracted to women in that way, I couldn't even identify what I was feeling yet. But I was drawn to look at her face, to decipher something I didn't yet understand. When they told me she would be directing the series, I was surprised. From her CV, I'd imagined she'd be older. She didn't even look thirty yet, but wasn't a young girl either—her voice low and confident as she explained her vision for the show with a poise few directors have, saying only what was necessary so as not to limit her work down the line. The entire time she looked at me but also at the whole team, with a thoughtfulness that is hard to come by. I also noticed her unique accent, which sounded somewhat American but a bit softer. She had a good sense of humor: when I stressed the importance of sticking to the timeline, she assured me I had nothing to worry about, she just needed to confirm the otters agreed to follow the schedule from my spreadsheet. I left the meeting without a delivery date for the project, which had never happened to me before.

9

Even in their dreams children are more carefree than adults. I've taken care of a lot of them, and they all move in their sleep in the same way, tossing and turning from side to side, and they become quieter and quieter as they grow, like they learn to keep their dreams inside the limits of their bed. Cora's not there yet, and must be dreaming about ballerinas right about now, as she moves and spins in my lap, pushing me to the corner of the seat. And now she must be thanking her audience in her dreams, while she leans forward, her face touching the window. I push her little shoulders back to the seat. I can't stand seeing my Chickadee with her mouth open like that, exposed to all the germs from the bus. I clean her face with a wet wipe. I don't mind this kind of thing so much anymore, but there was a time when this drove me crazy. I even thought I could see the germs, not just one individual germ but many many of them, so I cleaned myself, and cleaned Corinha, disinfected everything in front of us. After Lauro left, I stopped doing this and started seeing other things, both big and small. I hadn't noticed before, but anyone can see if they pay attention that the world is full of couples, big and small. The flower and the bud. The main house and the guest house. The plate and the saucer. Animals and their babies. And people, people are even worse. Everywhere I see the couples of big and small people next to each other, and I think I only noticed them now because I wasn't part of it anymore. They reminded me that every month I bleed, I continue to be a big piece on my own, standing by that painting on the wall, of a bathroom all covered in blood. Every time I looked at it, I felt this pain in my stomach, because to me the painting was a warning. You'll bleed again, Maju. You'll die alone.

Then I remember another opportunity I missed, Neide's boy. She offered me her baby so many times. From the moment she found out she was pregnant, that slut. Because she really was a slut. I actually met her because of her sluttiness, at Buenos Aires Square. In the middle of the white army, she was the only one wearing a color, reading a book while she watched a child. I came close to her because I also like to read. I walked by slowly to see the title of the book, from the Hot Desire Series. We ended up becoming friends and I found out we liked a lot of the same things, especially reading romance, though I preferred the regular kind and she preferred the ones that had the chilli pepper under the title. Neide was like this with books and with everything else. Maybe that's why I liked her so much. While the other nannies were busy competing against each other, look, this child is already bilingual, this other one went skiing in July, as if the children were theirs and not their bosses', Neide thought about making love. Every time I looked at her, like clockwork, she looked like she wanted to be reading or swaying her hips in front of the doormen with the boss's kid in tow. One day I even told her: Neide, woman, doesn't this kid complain about pacing all day in front of the Maison Blanche doorman? The boy must think there is some treasure buried there, so much they worked that sidewalk in front of the building. At the time, she already had Raquelly, who was around seven. She was Neide's first pregnancy, by a construction worker who went back home to the Northeast before she even started showing. My poor friend, she told me she was shaking when she told Mrs. Andreia that she was pregnant. And then a big surprise, she said Neide may keep her job. That she was going to make the other maid, the one she shared a room with, to work only during the day and go home at night, so she had space for the baby. As long as Neide worked nights, of course, because Mrs. Andreia had hired them to work around the clock for a reason. Though I thought there wasn't actually a reason at all. Who needs two maids in the middle of the night? Only Mrs. Andreia, the one who also needs a maid standing at the edge of the pool to hold her caipirinha, to make sure the kids won't knock it over—and not for the sake of the kids, for the drink's. I saw this scene all the time at the club, a burning sun and Neide standing by the pool with a glass in her hand, just waiting for Mrs. freckles to stick her head out and suck on the straw. I thought this was unacceptable, but no way to tell Neide that, God forbid someone say something bad about her boss. Then came the second pregnancy, by Renan from Maison Blanche. Neide came looking for me with a pregnancy test in hand, the plus sign on the display. I remember I said: Neide, you stupid woman, then patted her on the back and gave her a hug, because the poor thing was crying so hard her shoulders were shaking. Neide was sure it was Renan's, but he said no, better it wasn't his, because he was married, a father of three, she'll see what will happen to her if she shows up with a bastard kid to ruin his family. Neide panicked, because of course Mrs. Andreia wouldn't accept a second child into her home. She would have to find another job, go live in Capão, ask a neighbor to watch her kids. But then she got to thinking about Raquelly, how that move would change the girl's life. She'd have to leave the private school Mrs. Andreia paid for her, stay alone at home taking care of the baby, eight-years-old and already taking care of a baby, and out of Neide's sight. She was sure that by twelve the girl would already be hopping from man to man, like mother like daughter. So Neide decided it was better to have one healthy kid than two unhealthy. She'd give away the baby. Since she didn't have any family, only some distant cousins in Espírito Santo, she offered it to me, but I didn't want it. At the time I was trying to have my own Laurinho. Then the story gets worse, because Neide decided to hide the pregnancy. At first it was easy, her uniform was an oversized frock, her stomach fit perfectly under her front pockets. But then Neide started to gain weight, not only because of the pregnancy, but because as she got close to having to give the baby away, she started to crack. She picked baby names on a Monday, Rodrigo, Brian, Marcelo, then the next day looked for a place to leave the baby as soon as it popped out. All while stress-eating peanut candy. She had to tell Mrs. Andreia that she had a problem with her hormones, that one where your glands are tired. To Raquelly, who saw her naked, she said the same excuse for her big belly, and that all the crying in bed was from the pain. But children know everything. She said that Raquelly caressed her watermelon and cried too, without saying a word.

Then one Monday morning at around ten, the contractions started. Neide wanted to go to Santa Casa, but the other maid had left on vacation and she was all alone with the children. She had to give them their lunch and put them on the school van. When the van left, at ten to one, Neide had cold sweats and realized there was no more time to go anywhere. She lay on the floor in the laundry room and gave birth right there, cutting the umbilical cord with a pair of fabric scissors. Since her plan was to leave the baby at the hospital, she wasn't sure what to do, and she had little time to figure it out, because Mrs. Andreia came home with the children for dinner at seven. She called me and asked if I really didn't want to keep the baby. Then she waited for the pain to get a little better. When she felt a bit stronger, she went through the next steps: she bathed the little boy, put him in a onesie, clipped his pacifier to his collar. She squeezed out as much milk possible and put it in a baby bottle. Then she went after a bag. She wanted the finest one she could find, not in the sense of being sturdy, but in the sense of being *fine*, of giving her son the best she could with this single chance she'd have to give him anything, a plastic bag wouldn't do, they're too cheap. She rejected the grocery bags and the paper bags, the ones too small, too long, that had a smell, or were dirty, or girly, or flimsy, and one which was pretty good but had Ricardo Almeida written on the logo, which might make it seem like this was the baby's name. Until she found the perfect one: big, made of thick paper, soft bottom, rope handles, a pretty pattern, and some phrase written in English.

She stayed with the baby for as long as possible. Then she took the elevator down with her heavy bag, the diapers and bottle in it too. With her head down, she walked by the doorman, outside his building, walked two blocks to Rio de Janeiro Street and left the bag there, under a tree. She walked for a bit longer, then hid between a bush and a bench. She wouldn't leave until she saw someone find the baby. About ten minutes later a man noticed the bag, maybe the baby made a noise, Neide didn't know, she was too far to hear. The man crouched down, peered inside, grabbed the bag with his hand under the bottom, which Neide appreciated, that was a thoughtful touch.

At nine o'clock, she was already cleaning the dinner table when she saw it on TV. She couldn't believe it, it was her on the *Jornal Nacional*. The image from a street camera showed Neide walking with her head down, carrying the bag. Then a police officer showed the boy wrapped in a blanket and a reporter saying things she didn't understand, because she was nervous and also so focused on the baby, trying to see if he wasn't scared by all of this. That night it was Neide who asked to sleep in Raquelly's bed.

The next days, my friend walked around the neighborhood with her head down, to hide from cameras and to hide her tears. She thought the worst was behind her, and maybe it was, but problems also come in couples, big and small. Four days later, while walking on Rio de Janeiro Avenue again, Neidinha saw two security guards staring at her. Soon one went to her with handcuffs, saying she was under arrest for child abandonment.

They said they recognized her from the cameras, by noticing how this woman who kept walking by that street kept her head down in the same unusual way as the mother who abandoned the baby. At the police station, she found out that the baby had been sent to Child Protective Services, while she was sent to jail, where she stayed for two days. When she left, the sidewalk was thick with nosy neighbors and reporters, people yelling: you're a madwoman, why did you do this? Neide said she thought about Renan, about Renan playing sudoku by himself in the silence of the lobby. And without even knowing what she was saying, she yelled: despair, despair.

After Lauro left me, I thought about this a lot. I regretted not taking the baby, I thought it would have been better for me, for the baby, for Neide. But now, looking at Cora next to me, this way is best. If I had taken the baby, I wouldn't be touching my Chickadee's hair right now, going back to Mandaguaçu, and feeling happy like a child who can't yet stay inside her bed.

10

I was used to going to shoots in the cities where artists lived: São Paulo, Rio de Janeiro, Recife, Paris, Tangier, and even Tarsila do Amaral's Capivari or Candido Portinari's Brodowski. But now I needed to go where the alligators were. Everything was so new to me that I didn't even know what to wear. Out with the scarf I wore in air-conditioned studios and museums and in with what? At five in the morning, I somehow mustered the energy to try on some combinations of what I'd packed: ditching the button-down shirt because it looked too formal and the vest full of pockets because it looked caricatured. I finally settled on sweatpants, a t-shirt, and a pair of sunglasses that concealed my exhaustion while also making me a picturesque figure, as I watched the sun rise through the expensive blackout curtains, in front of a hotel in Corumbá.

The driver showed up soon after. It's two hours to get to Nhecolândia, he told me, and the name of the town sounded more absurd than ever, making me feel like I was still dreaming, cradled by the orange of the horizon. I thought of making the best of that time, I could sleep on the way to the town, or at least watch the dull morning landscape pass by, but my phone was already buzzing with emails from the gringos in Los Angeles who worked in another time zone and made me wake up every day with an overflowing inbox. I only took my eyes off the screen when I felt we were getting close, as we drove through the gate.

Our accommodation consisted of one bedroom with four

mattresses, a bathroom, and a porch with a rustic wooden table. I threw my suitcase on a mattress, next to the bags that were already there. I noticed the room didn't have AC, not even a fan, which made me mad at the cheapskate who signed on such a low production budget for this show. Me, in this case. At any rate, even if I had raised the budget, where would we stay? There was nothing better in the area, no hotel bar where I could have a drink, so I tried to focus on what lay beyond the window.

On the way to the shoot we passed by some ponds, which, according to our driver, in the Pantanal area were called "baias." They were deep indents in the ground where water accumulated, forming shapes like drops and hearts. We parked by the tip of the deep green heart-shaped pond, where I quickly spotted the director, who I hadn't seen since the meeting, with her eye in the camera lens, the lens nearly in the water. Her hair was pulled back in a loose bun, her lips parted, as she admired something she was seeing. Next to her, there was another camera, operated by a woman with a shaved head and big hoop earrings, who I assumed was the director of photography. With them was a young guy, so young he made me nervous, making me worry if he was old enough and had the proper permit to handle that sound equipment. But I forgot all my worry when Yara looked up from the camera, smiled at me and nodded in a friendly way, only to quickly put a finger over her lips to signal we had to be quiet. Her eye turned back to the camera. I stood there, waiting for a moment to introduce myself to the rest of the team.

Fifteen minutes went by and nothing. Yara, the DP, and the sound technician didn't move. They were so still for a moment I had the feeling they were three wax figures taken from Madame Tussauds and placed in this strange setting. I finally decided to sit in the shade of a tree, where I replied to all my unread emails and messages, until I realized that a whole hour had gone by since I'd arrived there. I looked up and saw that something had finally changed. The DP and the sound technician were in the same spot, but Yara was gone. I looked around and no sign of her. Then I heard the sound of rippling water, and out of it came the director, camera in hand. She ran to the shore, gesturing for me to come closer. She quickly introduced me to Herta and Felipe, placed the camera monitor in front of me and said: the romance scene you wanted. Two alligators were swimming to each other in the water, the bigger one lying and twisting over the smaller one, who I assumed was the female. They stayed that way for a few minutes, until their bodies separated again. Doesn't it look great? she asked, her eyes locked on the screen. Indeed, it did. The aggression of the alligators completely disappeared in the gentleness of their movements underwater, as if there truly was love there, and love could make acrobats out of clumsy creatures. Yara was dripping wet next to me, and that also caught my eye: the fact that she didn't mind that muddy water running from her hair to her face, while she watched the scene for the second time. After that, she left the camera with Herta, excused herself, and went God knows where.

I tried to make conversation with the bald woman, asking her what she thought of the shoot. She gave me a thumbs up: gooood, she said stretching the word out that way, and she smiled. I asked if they had managed to capture a lot of images the day before. There went the thumb again, without a word. Then she put her hands away in her pockets and kept on smiling, leaving me with the impression she suffered from some kind of mental disorder or maybe was one of those eccentric artists, with a sharp eye for aesthetics but a bit slow with everything else. I decided to talk to Felipe, who said the previous day had been very productive, but refused to add any details, just went back to his microphones, clearly intimidated by my higher position, a reaction I was used to.

Much to my relief Yara reappeared, with dry clothes, wringing her hair. How's the monologue? she asked and laughed, and quickly told me Herta was a fantastic DP, but spoke neither Portuguese nor English. They had met in Romania, filming bison in the Carpathians. Yara was impressed with how Herta captured light, a dense and melancholy light, much closer to cinema, to what she'd seen in Kusturica's Serbian movies. I liked what she said, I loved that director.

Then she showed me some scenes they'd shot the previous day. A female alligator swam in a pond with two hatchlings. At one point, the mother and the bigger hatchling swam away from the smaller one. Another alligator came into the scene and ate it, scattering pieces of meat everywhere in a matter of seconds. What's this? I asked, surprised. Hunger, Yara responded nonchalantly, as if that act of cannibalism were a normal part of life. And it was, for that species. Like Yara told me, it wasn't unusual for male gators to eat their own kind, including hatchlings. Unfortunate for the babies but convenient for me, and the narrative we wanted to dramatize, because it showed that alligators could also be their own villains. I shared this thought with her, thinking it was brilliant, and commenting that we already had scenes of villainy, conquest, romance, compassion, but I still missed other emotions, like anger. And how do you expect me to show that? Yara asked. Through the alligator's facial expressions? I guessed. Alligators don't have muscles on their faces, they don't have facial expressions. They're like . . . Bruce Willis. I let out a laugh. She continued: I didn't say this at the meeting because I couldn't, but I think this idea of humanizing animals is pretty silly. I was surprised. It was rare for one of my employees to address me so bluntly. Don't worry because I'm a professional, I'll do what you asked me to, but I wanted you to know that the beauty of wild animals is exactly in how they don't suit our expectations. At this point she took a joint out of her pocket, right in the middle of a workday, lit it, and even offered it to me. Of course I didn't accept. I was more in the mood for a Klonopin by then, given how my neurons were buzzing—half of them worrying about our angle for the series, the other half firing up thanks to my hormones. I pretended all was well and said she might know a lot about animals and directing, but when it comes to producing entertainment, I have the experience. The series had already been sold with that premise, and if the channel had invested two million, it was because that angle was appealing. But of course we could make the form a bit more flexible, we could talk about it. We have a lot of talking ahead of us, she said with a mischievous smile.

The local producer of the series showed up, bringing sandwiches and drinks. I mixed some of my fiber supplement in my juice, while Yara and Matuto talked about a local farmer. She asked after some guy named Norberto, as I wondered how it was possible she already seemed to know all the local residents. In that moment, my phone rang. The gringos above the equator had woken up. I replied to some emails, watched some scenes of another production in progress, and when I looked up again, the team was at the edge of the heart-shaped pond. Suddenly, an alligator burst out of the water, its front paws dragging its fleshy accordion body to the earth. Others came following. Alligators of all sizes emerged from the water, as if responding to a bugle call only they could hear. There were so many I thought the line of alligators would never come to an end, that they would keep coming out of the earth's throat through the pond's mouth until they filled up the whole planet. But of course that wasn't the case. Soon the line went thinner and I realized it was only the alligator population answering the call of another kind of bugle, the sun's. Basking in the sun. Or "lounging," as Matuto put it. In the end, it was a beautiful sight, the mountain range of spiky backs, nearly motionless around the lake. The team was so intent on capturing everything, even I got up and took a photo to send to my CEO.

A while after, I heard Yara screaming: it's her. And then: quick, the snare pole. Matuto ran to the spot with all our equipment, grabbed a long stick with a big hoop at the end, and handed it to Yara. With the contraption in hand, she moved toward a lone alligator at the edge of the pond. Herta and Matuto stood behind Yara, like they already knew—as they probably did—what she was up to. Crouched down, she moved slowly, until she got very close to the gator, lassoed its mouth with the cable, sealing it shut and eliminating any threat. Only then did she touch the alligator. She pressed her hand between its eyes. Slowly. And cried. I know because I saw her wiping her tears with the back of her hands. Then she let go of the release knob, and with a swift motion, she freed the animal. It was a scene right out of a thriller or an adventure show, except this was real life, in twenty-four-hour episodes, raw, unedited reality. As such, before we reached the climax and I could ask Yara about her relationship to the alligator, I had to go spend the rest of the day quite uneventfully: the drive back, the quick cold shower, the struggle to make my bowels move with people waiting on the other side of the door. When we finally sat down to eat, it was already dark. The symphony of animal sounds outside enriched the experience beyond what any image could have captured. I made myself comfortable among those sounds, while also savoring the crackling of the fire, as Matuto roasted a pig for us. We sat near him. Me, Yara, Herta, and Felipe. Herta, as usual, seemed aloof, not because of the language barrier, that can always be overcome, but because she seemed to enjoy staying in her own world, or rather, in our world, fully and without interlocutors, connected to something I couldn't see but which seemed nice, and which seemed to get even better as the Romanian woman sipped her bottle of 51. This one loves cachaça, Yara said. Sometimes I think she only comes to work in Brazil so she can drink it. I asked if they always worked together. Yara said whenever possible. In addition to being a wonderful professional, Herta came from a Romani family. She could handle the nomad life of making documentaries. And you, where are you from? I asked, still intrigued by her accent. From a town no one knows, Las Cruces. New Mexico? I asked. She looked at me, surprised. How could I not know it? It's home to the world's best enchilada, I said. Yara burst into a loud laugh. How did you end up in Las Cruces? I told her that I loved to travel. That I didn't travel more only because my husband was a homebody, I had a small daughter, and an executive role that tied me to the office, but in the past I had produced travel shows. In one of these productions, I had passed through Las Cruces, where we shot the three-meter-long enchilada, which, when laid out, looked more like a trampoline covered in sauce. I remember I also got footage of the fiesta's mascot, the chili pepper in boots, big mustache, and sombrero, what's it called again? I think it's Twefie, Yara answered, excited to remember that place. Then she told me she had left the town when she was very young, at just six years old. Her father was a biologist and her mother an anthropologist, they were only in Las Cruces because of her mother's PhD. After that, they lived in various cities and countries, going after her father's animals and her mother's people. I've also moved around, I told her. But for less glamorous reasons: my father had problems with drinking, gambling, and owed money to too many people. When things got complicated my parents would decide it was time to get a new start some other place. Sometimes I think that's why I like movies so much, because when I didn't know anyone in a new town, I went to the matinees and the movies kept me company. Yara leaned toward me. What a coincidence. I also went to the cinema when I felt lonely, that is, when the town had one. Though I don't mind the nomad lifestyle anymore, I got used to it, I don't think I could live any other way. She was going to say something else but Matuto interrupted us, serving pork with bread and passing to Yara a gourd in the shape of a horn. She drank from it and passed it on to me. Have you ever tried tereré? I said I hadn't. She explained it was a kind of iced yerba mate. Then she poured me some water mixed with the mate leaves in the bottom, again leaving me with the impression that she was very familiar with that place, that culture.

We started talking about food, of how delicious the pork was. While we ate, I tried to answer some emails. Until I smelled something. It was Yara smoking a cone joint, the cherry glowing bright-red in the night. She offered it to me, and once again I declined. It was still business hours, only three o'clock in Los Angeles. Herta also said no, she was satisfied with her cachaça. Matuto grabbed the joint and started talking about a boat that had sunk nearby, in the Chacororé pond, back in the eighteenth century. The vessel became well-known because local folk swear they can see the stern come to the surface during the full moon, and they can also hear the voices and laughter of the crew. That's just a legend, Felipe said. Matuto responded: it might be, but the boat is real. He'd been down there with a group of divers, saw it with his own eyes. The structure was all rusty, making the boat look like a castle from another world, and the fish brought life to everything, coming out of every window, every little hole. I glanced at Yara out of the corner of my eye. She was crouched down, her lips parted, like a child waiting for the next page of a book. Herta was also paying attention, and I had the strange feeling she could actually understand perfectly well. Matuto passed the joint to Felipe, who asked him about the sounds down in the water. A dog appeared and lay down next to Yara. She started to pet it. Have you been here before? I asked. She smiled that way again, mischievously. Why do you ask? You even know the dog. She laughed. I've never seen this creature before. But yes, I've been here a few times, she said. Then she sat down on the ground, facing me. She told me she spoke Portuguese and knew Brazil well because her mother was Brazilian. And also because her father was an expert in alligators, and he would come here all the time to study the caiman, Bruce Willis's scientific name, the Pantanal's alligatoridae. She told me that this reptile was her father's life. While other humans run away from them, she and her father had spent their whole lives going after them. That's why they'd lived in Florida, Australia, Egypt, Tanzania, and also in Corumbá, where he conducted his research. Now I understand your relationship to that alligator, I said. You certainly seemed to know him. Her, she corrected. And then added that she wasn't just any female. She was called CAI-3, because she'd been the third caiman recorded in her father's study, thirty-one years ago, around the time Yara was born. At the time, CAI-3 was also a baby, and would crawl over her father's feet, nibble on his toes. Her father followed her nearly every day, until she reached one meter twenty. Yara has some memories from then. Her father would tickle under CAI-3's mouth and she would close her eyes. They went back to Las Cruces, and by the time they came to the Pantanal again, CAI-3 had already grown to almost one meter eighty, and her father didn't even dream of tickling her anymore—he'd certainly lose a finger—but he continued taking care of her as he would a daughter. Or an amulet. While other alligators were dying, preyed upon by other animals or by disease, CAI-3 stayed strong, getting regularly jabbed at the lab. Much of her father's debt to CAI-3 came from the amount of theses he managed to develop with samples from her. Of course it wasn't always easy. Once CAI-3 must have had PMS, Yara said, because her father took her out of the water, did an ultrasound, but before he could get the cable off her mouth, the alligator started walking away. This was a serious problem, because if CAI-3 went back to the water with her mouth tied shut, she wouldn't be able to eat and would die. So, Yara ran and sat on top of the caiman—they always did that when they wanted to immobilize the animal—but CAI-3 reacted. She turned around and squeezed Yara against the truck. She heard a crack, it was her bone breaking. After telling me this, she took my hand, slid it under the collar of her t-shirt and moved my fingers all the way to her shoulder, where there was a bony lump. She made me touch it slowly, all while looking into my eyes. I felt my body go soft, until I pulled my fingers away.

Yara continued, saying that the previous year her father had been diagnosed with cancer. Even while he was sick, he wanted to go back to the Pantanal for their *last dance*. That was how he put it: *it's gonna be our last dance*. Because CAI-3 was getting old too. That would probably be the last of the forty, fifty meetings between the two of them. Yara also went, and even though her father could barely walk, it was beautiful. To avoid having to immobilize CAI-3, they went at night, since headlamps stun the animals. Her father quickly touched his longtime partner, he went over his research procedures, feeling the texture of her skin, checking her temperature. Since caimans are no poodles, they soon left the creature alone and went home.

Yara looked into the distance, at a horizon that couldn't be seen, and continued. Her father had also wanted to come to Pantanal to say goodbye to life, so he wouldn't spend his last days on a white bed in a white room in a white building where the most significant bit of nature is a flower yanked from the earth and thrown into a small water bottle. And that must really have been it, her father wished to leave amidst the warmth of living things; soon after they arrived in Corumbá, he died. I didn't know what to say, but I looked at her with tenderness. That was why I wanted to start filming here, she said. I felt like it would bring us good luck. Right in that moment, my phone rang. I put it on silent and asked about her mother, where she'd been this entire time. She said her mother had disappeared when she was ten years old. She went to research a remote tribe in Peru and never came back. Her father thought she'd been killed by squatters, but Yara thought she was still alive. That she'd wanted to disappear. And you? she asked. Tell me about you. My phone rang again and this time I couldn't ignore it, it was Matthew asking if we could do the last call of the day. I excused myself and went to talk to him.

When I got back to our room after the call, everything was quiet, the door shut. I opened it carefully so as not to make any noise. I imagined the crew must already have been asleep. And most of them were. Felipe was fast asleep on the mattress closest to the door and Herta next to him. Yara was changing, her back to me. She must have noticed me come in, as the door creaked softly, and my steps dragged slightly, but she didn't turn to face me, didn't even interrupt what she was doing. The only change I felt was that she seemed to slow down her movements, provocatively taking off her shirt and letting me see the profile of her breasts while she reached down to pick up another shirt, which she put on with the same slowness, until the loose, long fabric covered her butt cheeks. Then she turned to me and whispered: good night. I said good night back and grabbed my things to go to the bathroom, since I didn't feel comfortable changing in front of her. In there, I went over my extensive nighttime routine, from creams and vitamins to real needs and vices. When I got back to the room, Yara was also asleep. I turned off the lights and lay down on the only mattress left, between her and Herta, but I couldn't sleep a wink. I groped for my toiletry bag and grabbed a Klonopin.

When I woke up, still drowsy because of the pill, all the mattresses were empty. It was six fifteen. The driver must have already been waiting for me. We had arranged for me to leave at six and I couldn't miss my flight that morning. I quickly put on some clothes, stuffed into my suitcase whatever I had lying around, and left all disheveled, without saying goodbye.

11

I stop reading Nora's book before I reach the end. I don't want to be without a book on this trip, especially because I don't know how things will be like, God knows if people there have evolved, if they've opened any bookstores in Mandaguaçu. When I lived there, a man drove from farm to farm selling books, I remember. I already liked reading back then, but there were only war books, barely any romance. He also had some poetry, but I never liked those, I feel like people write verse when they're too lazy to fill the whole page. I take another sip of my sugar water and use a picture of my Lady to mark where I stop reading. Then I look at my watch, four o'clock, the bus must be stopping any minute now. And of course we'll get out. I'm like an armadillo, I can't see a hole and not go inside to check it out.

Wake up, Ana, I nudge my Chickadee. We'll be getting off soon. She rubs her eyes and asks where we are. I say: Santa Cruz do Rio Pardo, which I saw on the gas station sign. As soon as the bus stops, we get up. The passengers in the regular seats stand in front of us. It's the stress of sitting for so many hours on that hard bench. Cora pulls my hand. I want to go on the swings. I explain that we can't, we only have twenty minutes. She begs: please, just a little. I take pity on her. Just five minutes, not a second more. She looks at me, says: today is the best day of my life, and bolts out with Bibi.

Later she asks me to push her on the swing. I pull her all the way back first, because I know how she likes it to go real high. I watch the crown of her head coming and going and think maybe being a mother isn't so hard. People complicate it because that's just what they do with everything, but that's all there is to it, pushing a kid all day long until they don't need pushing anymore. I can do this push and pull all day. I don't know why but swings squeaking make me happy, but we don't have much time. Come on, Ana, your five minutes are up. She answers to the new name, what an obedient girl. Though obedient isn't exactly the right word: the little thing gets down from the swings and runs to the slide, only once! she yells out, as she goes into the tube. What am I supposed to do, fly like Wonder Woman and yank her out of it? I wait, tapping my foot on the fake grass, until the little rascal comes out. As soon as she appears, I grab her hand and drag her to the store. We pass by the counters, by the shelves, by a pile of candy made with calf's foot jelly which makes my mouth water. I even think of getting one but change my mind, it costs an arm and a leg. I grab a bag full of bread. I stop at a table, pick up little sachets of mayonnaise and ketchup, then we go to the checkout line. I did everything to avoid the candy aisle with my Chickadee, but now they're all here on the shelves by checkout anyway, a whole wall of sweets and gum on each side tempting us weak fools, the girl's eyes wide. I know Corinha, she'll pick the most expensive, some M&M's that come with a toy, a green ball with two glazed eyes and white rain boots. Can we get this one? she asks, and I stay quiet, thinking that twenty-eight reais is enough for a meal. Now I'm unemployed, can't go spending money on nonsense anymore. Chickadee starts to pout and I start to lose my patience too, because things have changed. I don't carry Mrs. Fernanda's bottomless money bags in my pockets anymore. It's hard, but I need to explain this to Cora. I squat down and look at my girl with warmth. When Maju gets money, she'll give you this whole store. But today Maju doesn't have any, I say, and I show her my wallet, empty because I keep all my money in my bra. The card, the smart-ass says, touching the plastic. I only have a bit of money there. Maju is poor, sweetie. She drops it. Can I at least have a gumdrop? I feel so much love for her, a love that goes through the walls of the store and beyond the roads out there. One for me and one for Bibi? That's when the two of us notice it, where's Bibi? We look at our hands, at my bag, which I open without much hope, I don't remember putting her there. A despair takes over our bodies. Hers because she can't live without the sheep, and mine because now is not the time to lose stuff, the bus is about to take off. I look at the time on my phone. We have five minutes. We bolt out of the store and, I don't know why, everything looks different now, a tangle of colorful packaging messing with my head. Help Maju out, where did you leave Bibi? She says she doesn't know, doesn't remember. We go through every place, it's not here, not here either. Until I remember the playground. The checkout line has grown, we won't have time to pay and also go look for Bibi outside. I leave the bread, yank the candy out of her hand. Maju can give you another one later, and we leave the store. I look for the bus, it's there with the others. We still have three minutes and people are always running late, we'll be fine, but we must hurry. We get to the playground. I look everywhere, I don't see the sheep. Cora crosses her arms. I won't leave without Bibi. Yes, you will, otherwise we'll miss the bus, I say firm, and pull Cora's hand. She lets go of my hand and grabs onto the climbing set, onto a metal bar where she sticks on her fingers with a strength I've never seen. No point in pulling her, they won't give way, I have to remove finger by finger, but as soon as I get her thumb and index finger she sticks them on again, ah how I want to slap this little girl. Let's go or I swear you'll get a spanking, I yell, and she cries, she's never heard me talk like this before. I feel bad, but now is not the time to feel anything. I kneel down to grab her, to hold her by the waist, then I see the sheep inside the slide tube. I run there and grab the damn thing. I give it to Cora, put the two of them in my arms, and run with them to the lot outside the store. The bus is gone.

12

I keep calling my sister. After a while, she finally picks up. She says she spoke to our mother at around five in the afternoon. It was a quick chat, because she was packing her car to go to the farm. Cora and Maju must have gone with her after all. This would explain her terrible departure time, during rush hour and as schools are letting out. At any rate, we can't be sure, and my sister, who was already planning to go to the farm the next day, offers to go early and leave in the next hour, promising she'll call as soon as she gets to the Hard Rock Cafe.

I tell Cacá. He says he'll take a shower and leaves his phone with me, in case anyone calls. I look at his screen; it's five past ten. I think it's time to make another drink. While I mix it, I see there's a new message from Yara and feel the same excitement I felt the first time.

It happened a few days after I got back from Corumbá. It was early; I was getting ready to go to work when I saw it: want to have dinner at my place tonight? I sat on the bed, unsure of what to reply. Of course I wanted to, but I didn't know if I should. Maybe I shouldn't, it was obvious this was trouble. But I hadn't felt anything like this in a long time, and why should I deprive myself of something life offers so rarely? I replied and started to think about the practical details, like my bikini situation. Then I grabbed my bag to go out, but couldn't get to the door. Cora clung to my leg. The more I tried to shake her, the tighter she held on. Unable to leave without hurting her, I said

I'd take her with me. She got up and said: today is the best day of my life.

That sentence softened me. Maybe because I already knew what the best day of her life would entail. The waxing place was in an old building on Angélica Avenue. On the ground floor, there was nothing besides the elevator and a sign pointing to the stairs. I don't know why, in all the years I'd been there, I always took the stairs. Maybe because I was in a rush, couldn't even wait for an elevator. And always being in a rush is in fact why I became a customer there. Unlike other salons, where you have to book an appointment, Audrey is always open, from eight in the morning to eight at night, weekdays, Saturdays, and holidays. A production line of hair-free women.

It was Cora's first time there. For someone who's recently come into the world, anything is an adventure, so much so she didn't mind having to climb up the stairs. Rather the opposite, she was excited to take two steps at a time. We got to the front desk and were sent to one of the booths. I started taking my clothes off, lying down on the table. Sara, with her name embroidered on her white coat, soon came in holding a big pot. She asked where it was going to be. Legs and bikini area, I answered, but I couldn't specify a style. What do women like? I quickly searched on the internet, only to confirm there isn't a consensus on anything. Something neat, in the shape of a triangle, seemed like a good call.

Sara stirred the pot with a wooden spoon. Cora asked to see what was inside. Sara told her to get up on the stool next to the table. My daughter followed the instructions, her curious eyes wandering over everything. Sara spread the wax on the left side of my groin, outlining the first edge of the triangle. She waited for it to set for a moment and pulled it off. I screamed. It was the first time I waxed so close to the genital area. The closer to the clitoris, the more sensitive our skin. Turning to one side, with my eyes watering, I saw a petrified Cora. Why is she doing this to you, mom? To remove the hair, I said in a choked voice. Sara showed her the big amber-colored piece in her hand covered in hundreds of bristly hairs like a strange insect captured in resin. To ease the pain, the beautician slapped the reddened area. Why do you let her do this, mom? No matter how hard I tried to explain cultural traditions, I didn't have an answer. What argument could be more compelling than the scream coming from the next booth, making that place seem like a lunatic asylum at the service of masochists outside and sadists inside? While Sara prepared another spoon, Cora whispered: will I have to do this one day? I said no, only if you want to, and this seemed to calm her down. After the beautician spread the hot wax again on the same spot, to remove some remaining hair, Cora held my hand and said: it'll be O.K., mom. I smiled at her. I stared at the ceiling as I waited for the wax to cool down, wondering what I was getting myself into by accepting Yara's invitation, because once we open a door, we can't control what comes in. I knew that the second wax application wasn't going to hurt as much, so when I asked Cora to repeat her words, it was a request for my emotional and not physical skin. Can you say that again, sweetie? It's going to be O.K., mom.

13

Give me a moment to believe this is really happening, that things are really this bad. Give me a moment for everything to sink in. I look from side to side, wonder if the bus didn't just move to another parking spot, if it's not still driving out of the parking lot. But of course not, the bus did what it had to do, get on the road at the scheduled time. It's not their fault you're an idiot, Maju. And then comes the worst part: I realize our suitcase stayed there. I want to cry as I remember everything on the bus, Cora's clothes, how will I manage with this girl with nothing to wear, without a single pair of underwear? And I without a brush to fix my hair? The little plastic forks, the packets of salt and sugar, those I can find again, but Nora's book . . . Now I'll never know what happened to Rosalind's romance. And that's not even the worst, it's the picture of my Lady that I left between the pages. But at least I have our documents and money. I pat my bra and feel the bills inside. Maybe I'm not a complete idiot after all, but still I want to cry. Thinking that I have nothing in this world except for my purse, I feel like passing out right there, on the empty parking spot where my Chickadee and I are standing. I only stop myself from falling on my knees and sobbing because I can't afford that, I need to figure out what to do next. Where's our bus, Maju? she asks. It left, but we'll figure it out, I say, trying not to pass my desperation onto her.

I look at the convenience store. I see a man in uniform. He must be a cashier on his break or a security guard, maybe he's been there this entire time though I didn't notice. Before going to talk to him, I tell Cora not to open her mouth, I'm afraid she'll mention her mother, that she'll give him any reason to suspect of something. I fix my hair and walk toward him, good afternoon, can you please help me? The man is nice, almost smiles. I explain the situation to him. He tells me this company has been doing this for a while, leaving passengers behind, the drivers get fired if they show up late at their destination. I tell him about my luggage. My eyes well up and I try to hold it. He says not to worry, because they'll keep my luggage safe. I doubt it, considering the kinds of people passing through bus stations, someone will probably steal it. But what I really want to know is how to get to Presidente Prudente. Good question, the man says, and scratches his head. Then he tells me there's a Cometa bus later that day that goes there, but that's a different company, they won't let me on board. There's a Garcia bus that goes to Maringá. He says I need to explain my situation to the driver and he'll let me in. From Maringá it's not difficult, you just buy a ticket right there at the bus station and travel a little more to Presidente. I think it's a good plan. I ask the man when this next bus is coming. He isn't sure, more than twenty buses stop there every day, but he knows it's later in the afternoon.

I do the math, leaving some room for error. We have half an hour to go to the restroom and stop by the store. After that, we must stand in the parking lot to wait for the bus. I crouch down, tell Ana what we're going to do, then we go to the restroom. While I hold my Chickadee so her butt doesn't touch the toilet seat, I think of my Lady. The same way I hold Cora, Our Lady of Aparecida holds me. I can't go on without her. I wash our hands careful and go into the convenience store. I walk to the shelf I saw before, between the stack of candy and the magazines. There are dozens of sacred figurines there, a divine perch. Gas stations know what's important to people: food, drinks, and divine protection. I look at the figurines one by one, Saint

Francis is cheap, cheaper than Our Lady of Aparecida, maybe because they took his vow of poverty to heart. What a miserable little statue he is, just a blob of clay, they don't even bother making all five of his toes, only outlined two, his feet look more like pig hooves. I won't take this one even if it's free, ugly as sin, it maybe even bring bad luck. I grab the Saint George figurine, look at the price, it's also cheaper than my Lady, and not so bad as Assisi. Cora looks at the knight with the sword and says: not this one, I'm scared of dragons. Standing on her tiptoes, she points at Mary and baby Jesus. Take this doll, Maju, it even has a baby. I like the suggestion. In terms of protection, it's a good deal, buy one get one free. And what a pair, the bosses of the whole thing. But eighty reais is too much, Chickadee. So take this one, please, take this one, she says, pointing at Our Lady of Fátima with three shepherd children and a sheep. The figurine is real beautiful, it fits in my purse and it costs okay, but suddenly I wonder what Our Lady of Aparecida will think of this. You pray your whole life to one Lady, you already have that channel open, like she's a friend you don't need to explain anything to anymore. You say the bastard's name and she already knows who it is, you mention an old fear and she knows what it's about, then suddenly, in addition to missing this intimacy, you're also betraying your friend. And all this because you wanted to save twenty reais. It doesn't look good. It's no wonder I'm loyal to my Lady. You know this one? I ask, showing Our Lady of Aparecida to Cora. This one is real cool. She even appeared in the sea to fishermen: there wasn't any fish in the sea and, after she showed up, they caught so much fish it didn't even fit on the boat. So take her, Maju. I'm still unsure, as soon as we can I'll have to buy us some clothes. I look at the price of my Lady again, at the sticker on the back of her mantle. Chickadee watches me. Then she pulls me down, looks into my eyes. When Cora has some money, she'll give you all the dolls, she says, pointing at the line of saints with her little finger. I feel that love again, a wave coming out of me, going through, and coming back to me again. And the love gives me courage. I think soon I'll be able to find a job, and I've always managed to find a way, there's nothing to fear, and I get the figurine of my Lady. Then I go after a bag of bread, a bottle of water, and one of juice. Before we go to the checkout counter, I casually lean against one of the tables, and grab napkins, sugar, some packets of mayo and ketchup. Then we go through the aisle for weak fools. I let Cora get a gumdrop, and pay. We sit on a bench in front of the bus stop, I know that's where the other bus will go because it's where our bus stopped. Also the parking spot is longer, a yellow rectangle on the dark road. I ask Cora if she's hungry. She says yes. Mayo or ketchup. Both, she answers, and I spread the sauce on a slice of bread with a drink stirrer I also found there. I chew my slicc and Ana chews hers. It's so nice to do something together in silence, and there's nothing but silence here in Santa Cruz do Rio Pardo, there's no bus coming, not a single soul around.

What now, what do we do? She asks as soon as she finishes her sandwich. It's the problem with kids of this generation, they think they have to be doing something at all times, as if living isn't enough already. I've told her plenty, when I was a child I stayed in the backyard of our house all day, not doing anything in particular, a worm crawling by was an event. Now it's different, kids need fireworks for life to be interesting, and there goes their mother to the mall to buy a rocket. I don't want that kind of trouble. I start telling Ana to stop that nonsense, watch life pass by, that little pigeon on the gas station sign. She looks, runs to the bird, it flies away. She comes back running. What now, what do we do? I say nothing. She asks for my phone and I give it to her, she hasn't asked for it in a while. We stay there together, cuddling, me sniffing her head still with that newborn smell, her watching cartoons, I don't know for how long. The Cometa bus to Presidente appears, other buses appear, and

I try to read the destination signs from far away, Apucarana, Marília, Penápolis. The security guard who wasn't a security guard, because he disappeared from the convenience store, was right about the bus schedule. The sun is almost going down when the bus to Maringá comes. I see the big letters right away and get up.

The driver's appearance comforts me. His belly leaves the bus before him, his round paunch, the number of ribs this man must have eaten, the damage he must do at a churrascaria. Someone who eats like that can't be bitter. He stretches, opens his arms, cracks his knuckles. The passengers get out. I tell Cora to keep quiet and we walk toward him. Sorry to bother you, Mr. . . . Josias, I say, reading his badge. I explain the situation, show the ticket stub so he can see we're not tricking him. He says he wants to let me get on . . . but there aren't any open seats. The day before a holiday on that route was complicated, the bus is always full. If there isn't any empty seat, imagine two, which is what you need. I say that's not necessary, she can sit on my lap. Or she can sit and I stand. He says that if he authorizes something like that and gets pulled over, he'll lose his license and his job. I don't know what to say, I stare at his shoes, all shiny, very polished. I wonder if since the bus left without us, maybe we can wait until the passengers get back to see if it's still full? He agrees, but it's unlikely he'll abandon any passengers, he's not irresponsible like the driver who brought us. Was it Solano? he asks, but I'm not sure. Then he tells me to wait, maybe a passenger will decide to stay there of their own wish.

We wait. I count the people getting back on the bus, though I don't know why, I have no idea how many seats the bus has, or how many passengers to expect. When a whole lot of people have already gone in, the driver looks at his watch, and gets on. I see him through the tinted glass, going down the aisle, looking at the seats on each side. Finally he comes out and yells: Maringá, last call. I hold the figurine of my Lady inside my purse. A woman comes running, holding one of those peanut candies that look like an elephant foot. The glutton goes in and the driver tells me it's full. I try one more time. I can squat, no one will see me. He doesn't say anything, but looks at me with pity. I seize the opportunity and plead with my eyes. What do I do now? He thinks for a moment. He says at night there's a bus to Presidente Venceslau, that can work, Presidente Prudente is on the way. But don't risk waiting for another full bus, get the tickets online. I show him my phone, it's dead. He seems to read my mind, because he doesn't insist anymore. He says to go to the town center. It's nearby, a twenty-minute walk down the highway. When I get there, I just need to find the shopping center and get the tickets.

14

I found it strange, dinner at seven, a little early for Brazilian standards. The place was also unusual. In São Paulo, people tend to prefer the safety of an apartment or a suburban house, but hers wasn't even hidden behind a wall, but behind a flimsy gate overtaken by ivy. I rang the bell. Yara appeared and kissed me on the cheek.

We went in. The room had barely any furniture, only an antique couch, with a worn fabric cover, a TV and a trunk between the couch and the screen serving as a coffee table. It's what you can do when you don't spend much time anywhere, Yara said. And pointing at the trunk: everything I own is in there. For real? I asked, thinking of the magnitude of my closet. She nodded. I thought you lived in one of those furnished apartments. It would make more sense, but then I wouldn't be able to have all these plants. Or have Paul and Lennon, she said, pointing at a fish tank in the little hallway between the living room and the kitchen. Those who can't have dogs make do with betta fish, she concluded, showing me her aquatic Beatles up close, while I thought about how I for one couldn't even take care of a fish. When I was eighteen, I got one and it died of starvation after I forgot to feed it for I don't even know how long. But I didn't tell her that, I didn't want to come off as insensitive, especially to animals, so I said: I love fish, then hoped she'd leave it at that, so I wouldn't have to add: grilled sole and salt cod à Gomes de Sá. Are these your favorite Beatles? I asked, changing the subject. They were, though now I like George better, but Paul and Lennon were my first fish, a pair of tetras I had to abandon in Miami when my father and I moved to Tasmania. Since then I've named all my fish after those first ones, as a kind of homage, she said, staring at the fish in the tank. Then she continued: though lately I've been thinking I probably name them so to feel like I never abandoned them in the first place, that inside these two are all the others. What a fate for these two, I said. And we laughed. Then we walked into the kitchen.

She pulled up a stool for me. And sitting on the other side of the counter, she said: what do you want to drink? I asked if she had any spirits. She said her bar was more of a cheap pub, the only spirit she had was a bottle of 51 cachaça Herta had left, but she had cold beer and a great bottle of wine from her last trip, would that work? I accepted the wine, taking a swig to help me relax, and so I'd stop behaving like the fifteen-year-old girl I'd suddenly turned into, staring at the braless breasts I could see through her shirt. I realized I hadn't been this obsessed with boobs since I was two months old, and with that thought, I downed almost the entire glass. She seemed more at ease than me, as she crushed a little pile of weed and another of mint on the same cutting board, while I wondered if I liked lamb. She was making koshari, an Egyptian dish that pairs well with this kind of meat.

Soon she offered me a joint: are you sure you don't want it? I said no and explained why, I still had my nightly call with my boss. I could handle talking to Matthew a little tipsy but not stoned. Though now that I thought of it I had already talked to him in all kinds of situations. Actually—I only told her this because the wine had loosened me up—I used to take these calls in the bathroom, sitting on the toilet, while waiting for a delivery from my worst colleague: my intestines. Yara laughed. You talk to your boss in Los Angeles while taking a shit? Not taking a shit exactly. Just trying to. And this time we laughed together. I realized my embarrassment had disappeared not just from the wine but also from the ease with which Yara carried herself, making me feel comfortable too. And the reason for this group activity? To save time. Time for what? I didn't know how to answer; truth was, lately, I didn't even have time to keep up with TV shows. Agnes, my right-hand woman, had been doing that for me. All this hurry was so I could squeeze as much time as possible to sink in the bathtub and relax a bit so I'd be able to sleep and avoid popping another Klonopin in the middle of the night. All these thoughts were just in my mind when Yara joined me on my side of the counter, standing really close to me and saying: I know how tough the life of an EP can be, I admire you for doing it. Then she kissed me. She held my waist and gently touched my breasts. I got wet to the point I wondered if I'd be needing adult diapers for the next date.

Yara went back to the saucepan, which was bubbling up. She lowered the heat. Then she started arranging the pieces of lamb on a skillet, placing the bones neatly in a row. I was amazed at the complexity of a human being who loves animals but also enjoys tearing them up with their teeth. As she went to get rosemary from a pot, my thoughts wandered back to the trunk. I tried to picture what was inside it. What an efficient way to get to know someone: through their trunks, the chosen essentials of their lives. We could see each other's trunks, the objects offering mutual discovery that no dialogue could provide, because unlike in a conversation, there would be no way to improvise common interests based on what the other had previously said. What would I find in Yara's trunk? I thought, maybe a camera, lenses, postcards, a pocketknife, maybe even a compass. And in my trunk, what would she find? A bottle of gin, a box of Klonopin, fiber supplements, a laptop, a cervical massager. Fuck, I used to be better than that. And feeling like the owner of a lame upper-class executive trunk, I saw Yara come back with the rosemary. She sprinkled it on the skillet and put everything in the oven. We were about to kiss again when my phone rang. It was Agnes, who wanted to discuss acquiring the rights to an image.

When I hung up, Yara was setting the table. I helped her, carrying the wine glasses, another bottle of wine, and the bottle opener. She checked the lamb, said it was ready, asked if she could serve it. She mentioned she usually woke up with the sun and was starving by that time. I agreed, only then realizing I hadn't eaten all day, anxious about our date. We sat down. I tried the food. I said it was delicious, even though it wasn't all that.

She told me she learned to cook out of necessity, alligators don't do take out. Also, it had always been a way of taking the places she'd been with her: she couldn't carry the clay pots of the Bedouins, but she could carry a recipe. I said I'd been dreaming of going somewhere so remote. Since Cora was born I'd only been to countries colonized by Starbucks. She asked why. I had to think before answering. Maybe the problem wasn't the place itself—if kids survive eating chili peppers in Mexico or drinking polluted water in India, why wouldn't mine? The real issue was how difficult I found it to fit Cora into my life. With an honesty that surprised me, I told Yara how I was struggling with being a mother. It was much easier for me to handle unpredictable weather on an open-air shoot in São Pedro than a child in the middle of a tantrum. Aren't you just supposed to let them cry? she asked. I have no idea, I said, and we laughed. I told her I was kidding, that I did know what to do, I just lacked the patience. She told me she wasn't always the most patient either, but she'd learned from her dad, who in turn had learned from nature. One time they stayed three hours and twenty minutes waiting for a broad-snouted caiman to come up for a breath of air. I told her I was happy to have found a monk like her to be part of the series. That I really liked the first cut of the episode and that I had loved both her work and Herta's. It really is good, she said. Then she rubbed her bare and rough foot against my leg. I felt a chill go up my spine, the whole machine coming alive again, like I'd learned in a documentary we'd made—testosterone giving me lust, adrenaline making my heart race, dopamine making me lose any trace of inhibition. I took off my shoes and climbed her calf with my five wormy toes. When I came to, we were standing, me leaning against the table, she kissing my mouth, and licking my neck. My phone rang again. I picked up and started to talk to Matthew, but she didn't move. She continued as she was, caressing my stomach. My call was important, I couldn't get distracted. I moved away, I kept backing off, until my back was against the wall, but she followed, her tongue tracing down my waistband, her fingers unbuttoning my pants. Stop, I told her, and heard a confused *what?* on the other end of the line. Matthew went on about a list of concerns with a series we were producing. His voice was a buzz in my ear as her tongue ventured through what was left of my forest; while he told me about a casting issue I was caught up thinking about my bikini wax, did it look alright? Then I let go of all thoughts, only saying *yes* to everything, and with each *yes*, she sucked even harder. Cut it out, Yara, I don't come with oral sex, I begged. But she ignored me and kept going and going, and while Matthew was telling me that an actor had to go on leave because of cancer, I climaxed. I came through oral sex, standing up, while my boss talked about bladder cancer. I had the urge to kneel down and offer Yara a medal made of my pubic hair, but of course I stayed on the line, entering a state of bliss that even led me to wonder about the emotional state of the actor struggling with cancer, and not only about our production's financial loss.

As soon as I hung up, I looked up at her and shook my head. Aren't you the one who likes to multitask? she asked. I nearly slapped that smiling face. This part wasn't covered in the documentary; why we feel like squeezing, crushing, killing our very object of affection. I grabbed her by the waist, thinking of doing to her everything she'd done to me. I slowly pulled up her T-shirt, but my phone rang again. I ignored the call for a while, but the nanny ended up wearing me down. Maju said that Cacá had forgotten to buy a birthday present for Cora's friend, and the party was the next morning. Would I maybe have time to buy something? I told Maju that I wasn't about to go after a gift at that hour. She said Cora didn't like to go to parties empty-handed, she was embarrassed. She asked if I couldn't stop by a newsstand, buy anything. All right, I said, to get rid of her, already whispering to Yara, who looked at me expectantly. I was about to hang up when Maju continued, saying that the present couldn't just be of any cartoon character; it had to be something for a little girl, like Peppa or Hello Kitty . . . or something else I didn't even hear, because right then Yara yanked the phone from my hand and threw it as far as she could. Are you crazy? I asked, watching the device soar in a shiny arc, turning into a firefly as it disappeared among the plants. I turned around and saw a smile growing on her face. Now we're finally alone, she said. And I caught myself smiling too.

We went up the wooden stairs that led to her bedroom. It was bathed in moonlight, the lonely moon of São Paulo, without constellations to keep it company. The light poured in through the balcony, falling on the double bed. Next to it, there was a spotlight from a film shoot, covered in an orange plastic sheet, but she didn't turn it on, which I liked. I was still a bit shy, because that was all so new to me, a body like mine, with breasts smaller than mine, with a groin that, if you can believe it, had never seen a razor or a single drop of wax, but otherwise all the buttons were in the same places. Even so, I wasn't entirely sure what to do. Suddenly, I was on top of her, touching her clit and wondering how many fingers I should stick in: one, two, three? Until I realized I shouldn't be thinking about anything, just letting things flow, and it felt more natural than ever before. With a man there's the inherent issue of speed, or at least an awareness of time. At some point he comes, and it's over. As nice as a man might be, this creates a hierarchy. Between us, time didn't feel linear. We moved in circles, playing, touching, coming, licking, biting, coming again. At one point I got up to go to the restroom and realized that I had come more times that night than in the past several months with Cacá.

When I returned, Yara had turned on the spotlight and turned it to the wall. The bedroom was steeped in a warm light. She got a joint out of I don't even know where and lit it. This time I took a hit just so I wouldn't look bad, but I didn't want to smoke much. I was feeling so good I didn't want anything to ruin it. How weird to need a fix just to feel good, constantly teetering between the highs and lows: anxious about work or exhausted from it, starving or stuffed, thirsty or drunk. It's like trying to find balance on a razor's edge, always on the verge of being cut in two. But in that moment I floated, wrapped in Yara's arms.

My phone, I only remembered a while later.

Do you want me to get it? she asked.

Better not. At this hour the only one who'd call me is my mother. And she only calls to nag, ask for money, or favors . . . Maybe I wasn't born to be a daughter either.

No one is born to be anything.

A beautiful sentence, if only it were true in the real world. You know better than me that all animals have their purpose.

I'm talking about moral expectations.

What do you mean?

You think you're a bad daughter? Did you know that the male Acarophenacidax mite impregnates his sisters while he's still inside his mother? Then the sisters kill the mother to come out.

And they're all born in time for Sunday lunch.

And even if they could feel guilt over this, they wouldn't.

One more example.

Some spiders and scorpions kill their mate after copulation. And the praying mantis not only kills her mate, but also eats his head.

I might even pray with her after this.

Have you seen it?

Not even on TV.

The praying mantis holds their mate's head like a glass of wine and sips the gelatin that overflows, she said with a vocabulary that caught my attention, because even though she'd been raised speaking Portuguese and had lived in Mato Grosso do Sul, as far as I knew she didn't use the language much. I was about to make a comment, but didn't want to derail the conversation. They wouldn't dare touch their own kids, though, I said.

Of course they do. You saw the alligator we shot in our episode. I don't know if it was eating her own hatchlings, but it's very common. Lions, who have no idea they're the kings of the jungle and wouldn't dream of their Disney reputation, sometimes kill their cubs only so the lioness will go into heat sooner. They don't have the patience to wait for nursing to be over before another quickie.

All this to convince me there's no heroism in the animal world?

Nah, I've already stopped caring about that. I'm doing the series my own way, she said with a malicious laugh, which made me unsure if she was serious or joking. I'm giving you these examples so you'll let go of your guilt. Including the guilt of being with me, because . . .

The bees in Botswana cheat on their mates with other bees.

Bees don't even mate, the queen is the only one who has to go through the effort. But some fish change their sex throughout their life . . . And female bonobo apes, which I consider to be the most evolved species on the planet, mate with males, but also have sex freely with each other.

Tell me more.

She expands on the scale of this stuff. I noticed "stuff" is the word she used when she couldn't find a better one. She continued: I witnessed something interesting when I was with the bonobos in Congo. A group of female bonobos went under a tree that had a big fruit, like a jackfruit, I'm not sure, and they stared at it uncomfortably, waiting to see who'd jump and eat first. I was expecting conflict, that it would get physical, she said pausing for a moment, as if picturing the scene.

Then what happened?

Well, it did get physical, but not the way I'd expected. They started to rub their clitoris against one another's. They were doing hoka-hoka, as I learned from the researcher who was with me.

But wait, what about the jackfruit?

They did that precisely because of the jackfruit. So they would relax, strengthen the trust between them and eat the fruit together. They do this all the time in stressful or competitive situations.

They eat the jackfruit.

That's right, she said, and we enjoyed ourselves at the thought that this method could be applied to businesses. That at a critical moment, the meeting would stop so everyone could take their clothes off, and come back relaxed, ready to address the issue.

She laughed loudly, then grabbed her joint again.

But wait, I said, while she lit it. Have you noticed the animal world subverts all rules except one?

She took a hit.

Everyone fucks everyone, fish change their sex, the bonobos couldn't care less that sex is only for procreation, but the mother role is never subverted.

Some mothers kill their own offsprings.

In what circumstances?

As far as I know, only when they don't recognize the baby as their own. Or if it's born with any anomalies. They prefer to feed the ones that have more chance of surviving.

I see . . . , I said. Then I got quiet, feeling the weight of that. I noticed Yara felt it too, she was probably thinking about her own mother, because her face dropped.

Come here, I said to her. Tell me more about this hook-hoka.

She looked at me affectionately, then smiled and grabbed me. We went on eating jackfruit for I don't know how long. Until we lay on our backs. What time is it? I asked. Four. I started to get dressed. Then we went downstairs to the garden because we still needed to find my phone. Yara grabbed a flashlight. I was a bit wary of getting into those bushes. I was afraid a frog or something might jump on my feet, but she gently took me by the hand. We moved forward, the light revealing the ground: roots, flowers, a yellow bucket. I looked at her and imagined her older and the same, childlike and eternal in her explorations, and I thought I would have followed her through many gardens.

The phone was under some leaves. Still working, by some stroke of luck. And with no missed calls. When I was about to head out, Yara asked when we'd see each other again, if I'd go with them to the shoot in Acre. I said I couldn't go because I had important meetings all week. She suggested I fly out on Friday night and meet her in Rio Branco. Didn't I want to leave the Starbucks circuit? We could have an amazing weekend in the Amazon, hosted by her Yaminawá friends. I only smiled and shook my head, without giving her or even myself an answer.

When I got home, I was careful not to make any noise. Still, Cora woke up, maybe because she wasn't sleeping soundly anyway. She needed to pee and asked me to take her to the bathroom. I sat her down on the toilet, watching her eyelashes fall, her eyes almost closed. After I wiped her, I took her in my arms, and tucked her in bed. She asked me to stay with her for a while. I sat on the sheets, among stuffed animals. I put her head on my lap and stroked her hair. Suddenly, I felt her sniff something. My pants, my thighs. She looked at me and said: you smell different, mommy. Like fish.

15

It's because of moments like this that I believe in God. Some people will say that if we missed the bus it's because He wasn't looking over us. But you can always look at it another way. If we get on the road before dark, it's because He is with us. At least I hope he is, because it's going to take more than twenty minutes for us to get to Santa Cruz—a four-year-old child walking is like an adult with one leg. I try to be patient, it's not right to rush a kid, the two little beans walking by my side in patent leather shoes, kicking pebbles. God is also in the road's divine providence, because it might as well have been a narrow road uphill, but no, it's a highway that cuts through a field, nothing on one side, nothing on the other.

There are no buildings for a few more minutes, until something appears. The gates to a castle, Cora perks up. And maybe because it's blue, she concludes this must be Arendelle. The entrance to Elsa's kingdom in *Frozen*. I know this isn't it, of course we're not in Arendelle, not even at Beto Carrero World and much less at Disney, poor people only have a right to fantasy in their sleep. But those three fluffy stems in the shape of a giant arc really look like an entrance to something, to nothing in this case, because there's nothing around it but bushes. Now I see a little hut, a simple white building with a door in the middle. Is that the castle? Ana asks and points to the house disappointed. That's not a castle. We go close, until my old and tired eyesight makes sense of the stems. They are the three brushes which I imagine once upon a time washed buses or trucks, given the height; now all the bristles fall apart, blue needles blowing in the wind. Near, I also see some abandoned gas pumps, old newspapers fly around, the door to the hut ajar, as if inviting us in. I decide to snoop, we have to pass by it anyway, what's the problem? We just can't take long so we won't leave after dark, I tell my companion, and push the creaky door.

I go in and find what I think was the office for that dump, I say dump because, wow what a sloppy crew. They sure left in a hurry, without a minute to pack up. On the wall there's a calendar with a bare ass, a stopped clock, a shelf with some dusty bottles of motor oil—I only know because Lauro was obsessed with this Havoline—and a low cabinet, and a cash register. I tell Cora don't touch anything, imagine the germs, then I open the till, just in case they left a bill behind. Of course not, if there's a fire and you have to choose between grabbing a change of clothes and money, most people will run naked through the flames no doubt. These bunch here were no different, they left everything behind except the cash; the only thing I find digging into the corners of the till is fifty cents. But then I hear a drawer open, and Cora saying: look at the treasure. I turn around to scold my Chickadee, I said don't touch anything! But then I see a drawer full of pearls, golden chains, colored stones. It's a lot, twenty, thirty pieces, of course all fake, as I learned from Neide, real jewelry is never that big, she herself only wears delicate little things to make it look like the gold is real. I crouch down to see, grab a heart pendant. Ana asks if she can put on a ring. I clean it, tell her now she can, and while she's distracted with the cheap emerald, I wonder what that plastic jewelry is doing there, in the drawer of an abandoned gas station on the side of the road. Maybe they sold these, but it doesn't look like it, the room doesn't have anything to display it in. I don't think they sold anything besides motor oil—if they didn't sell water or coffee, why sell girly paraphernalia at a truck stop? Maybe it belonged to an employee, but that's also weird, who has so much stuff and leaves it in a drawer at work and not at home? The ring Ana took is too big for her finger, I notice her spinning the stone, and that reminds me of something. Suddenly, I see Dinalvinha when we were eight, nine years old, holding a makeup bag to do my face. I remember the bag well because I was just starting to read, and while she put on eyeshadow, I must look down, and my eye fell exactly on the little color squares. I tried to understand the name written under each pan, but it was hard, probably in another language. I think I asked if the bag was her mother's, or I didn't ask anything but she wanted to tell me, I don't know. All I know is that while she put on green eyeshadow on my eyes, she told me she'd gotten the makeup bag from a trucker who came from Paraguay, that if she went in his truck and played this game where she took her clothes off, he gave her everything, and showed me a tube full of gum he'd also given her, and offered me one. Maybe this thought came because Cora was standing there wearing these grown-up baubles in front of me, or maybe because when I got home that time wearing makeup, my grandmother Brígida spanked me with a belt, made me promise I will never paint my face or go to Dinalvinha's again, and the pain from the whipping was so hard I never put makeup again, only lipstick when I was already with Lauro, the Sweet Poison. Is that why there was a drawer full of fake jewelry, so the truck-stop people can get women on the road, maybe little girl who showed up? This thought makes my stomach turn and I take it all off Cora, this is not for children. She pouts, but lets go. I will never wear them, but I'm not leaving them either. I grab it all, then I open the second drawer, I find a pen, a bottle opener, a receipt pad with carbon copy, and stick everything in my bag, you never know what the next day brings. Then I say: come on, Chickadee, and I'm not sure why, we leave through the back door, where I see an even uglier mess, weeds growing over old tires. I hear a sound and in the moment I think it's a snake. I grab Chickadee in my arms, but quickly realize the sound is coming from a bush where two ears stick out. I take a moment to understand what animal that is, because it has the head of a dog but the body of a sick foal, almost as tall as Cora, so skinny its ribs peek through the skin. It's a doggy, Cora says, and I see that she's right, but what a dog, an aberration of nature, in my whole life I've never seen a dog that big. I only don't run away because the dog looks more dead than alive, weakly getting up. Cora asks to get down, she wants to pet the dog. I've never seen a child who loves dogs more than this one, but I don't let her, even though the animal is barely strong enough to scratch its ears, I'm still a bit scared of it, of something evil in it I can't explain. Or maybe I can, because I've thought about this before, of how I'm afraid of small things. I'm not scared of what's over the top. I worked at a house where the son loved horror movies, I've watched more than I can count. He was terrified of that ugly doll, Chucky. My grandmother was also afraid of silly stuff like that, spirits hovering sheets. But not me, it's the little things that get to me, because in the same way God is in the small stuff, so is the devil. I've heard Satan in the bell chimes of a church near Mrs. Tarsila's house. The bell rang thirteen times at midnight. I even asked at the parish: what's wrong with the bell? The priest said nothing was wrong, that I was mistaken. I started to write it down, I waited until midnight to hear the bell, then kept tally on a piece of paper, it rang thirteen times every night. Another time I spotted the devil's horns: I had problems sleeping and saw on Facebook a maid from the neighborhood was posting photos. She started at one in the morning, pictures of her smiling in all kinds of places, the usual social media nonsense. The problem is that she didn't stop posting, by my calculations it was more than fifty pictures, one after the other until sunrise. By then what I saw wasn't happy anymore but crazy, all those images trying to let out something. And now this dog, the size of a foal, this weird beast, the devil doesn't send a messenger with red eyes or a fiery head. The dog walks in our direction looking like a normal dog, with puppy eyes, sniffing my pants. Ana says: can we keep him, Maju? I say we can't, it's too big, and I think: calm down, maybe that's all this is, a big dog, a lonely animal abandoned by someone who worked at the gas station and is still waiting for them to come back. I go inside again to see if I can find out how long he's been there, without anyone to feed him. I look at the pages of the calendar and see the date, December 23, 1998. Now it's not only the dog that scares me. How is it possible for everything to stay still like this for more than twenty years?

I hold tight onto Chickadee and get the hell out of that place. The dog follows and I say: *vade retro*, but he doesn't give up, I have to toss a slice of bread for him to stop trailing us. He leaves and I finally put Cora down, my arms can't take it anymore. Come on, Ana, let's go, and we walk for about ten minutes, until she complains that her feet hurt. At first, I don't pay any mind, I think she's just whining, but soon she complains again and stops walking. I feel like slapping myself, how stupid can I be, I put some brand new shoes on the girl, because I wanted her to look nice for the trip, and didn't even think they might hurt. Maybe I didn't think of it because I didn't imagine us walking this much and also because I packed other shoes in the suitcase, and now I have nothing, not even a band-aid to put on her heel, which is red, all peeled. I fold down the back of the shoes so it doesn't touch the blisters, but she can't walk good like that. The shoe slips out, I have to put it on again. She complains. I open my bag and grab a little sugar packet. I tear it open and say: suck on this, Ana, come with Maju and suck on this. Maybe this will help her calm down and forget about the pain, but then it doesn't do much, and a few moments later she starts crying again, it hurts too much. I think of carrying her again, but I can't handle it, and there's no sign of the town ahead. We sit right there, and I hope a city bus will pass by,

I'm sure not hitching a ride. We stay that way for a few minutes, Cora whimpering, and I staring at the sun go down like a golden coin falling in the horizon.

Suddenly, she pokes me. She points at a bright neon light and says: I want corn. The light is a ways away, I squint to see it. It's really an ear of corn, and on top of it there's a heart blinking and in big letters, Big Corn Love Motel. I tell her there's no corn there. She says there is, she can see it. I explain it's not a place for eating, it's for something else. She says at the ice cream place near home there's a big ice cream out front and there's ice cream inside, so there's corn here too. I tell her this is a place for couples, look at the heart, but she insists and starts to cry, I want corn, I want corn, and I look for the word to explain, but how can I tell her that's not really an ear of corn? I mean, it is. My God, that's some big corn. I think of saying boyfriends go there to plant a little seed in their girlfriends, men put kernels in the women's stomach, but that's not even true, men these days only serve wrapped corn, and that's not appropriate conversation for an angel her age anyway, so I just try to calm her down, look, here's your sheep, Chickadee, but she keeps crying, complaining about her feet, repeating: I want corn. I wonder, why not go there, show her there's no food and maybe ask for help, for them to call a cab, so we can find a way to get to Santa Cruz at some point.

I grab Chickadee, look at both sides of the road, and cross it quickly. It's strange how it's suddenly night, it seems that it's a different world on the other side of the road. Now with stars around the corn, the neon heart is like amygdala in the sky's throat. We get closer and closer, and I can already see the dump, people there can't even cut the grass, or maybe they like hiding all the cars passing through behind the bushes. I'm a bit uncomfortable, because I've never thought of going to a place like this, once Lauro and I even tried, but it was Valentine's Day, the line was so long, when it was our turn they were all out of the cheap suites, and we didn't think it was right to spend so much money to make love. And I learned something that day, which is that no one goes on foot to a place like that, especially not a middle-aged woman with a child.

We go through the entrance and stop at the booth. The woman doesn't notice us, she's looking at the computer, she must be used to listening out for cars. She jumps when I tap on the glass. And she jumps even higher when she looks at me then at the child I'm carrying. With my free hand, I pat down my hair and start to explain, we missed our bus, maybe she knows of a bus going to Santa Cruz do Rio Pardo? She says she lives in the opposite direction and rides a motorcycle to work, she has no idea. I ask if she can call a cab, and she says that's better, there's a cab company in town, just let me grab my phone. In the meantime, I put Chickadee down, I take a peek inside, the woman dialing with her big red nails. She tries a few times, I watch while she does it, she blows her bubble gum while she waits for someone to answer. Then says: there's no one there. I ask if we can wait there for a bit, if she can try again later. She says that sorry but we can't, that the motel's administration prohibits anyone staying out there, there are employees who were fired for letting the Avon lady stay for three minutes. I ask if I can charge my phone and says no, she isn't allowed to talk to anyone, let alone bringing other people's stuff into the booth. Cora pulls at my sleeve. Maju, why is it taking her so long to get me the corn? There's no corn here, I say, annoyed, and Chickadee starts to cry. I don't know what to do. As if that isn't enough, a car is coming in and I don't know if because she wants to help us or to get rid of us, the woman makes a suggestion. Why don't you book a suite, rest for a moment, charge your phone, give the girl some food? I'm poor, lady, I almost blurt out, but first I decide to look at the prices on the sign next to me. It's not as expensive as the motel in São Paulo, maybe it's really a good solution.

I'm a little confused because all the suites in that love dump are named after flowers, but the price has nothing to do with the plant. I see the Daisy Suite and think it's the cheapest, but it isn't, seems like Orchid or Colombian Rose are less pricey. The woman sees me struggle and says the last two don't have a hot tub but are really good, and the Orchid even comes with a bathtub, it's the best value, the most popular. I can't even think straight, because Cora is still screaming, I want corn with butter, I want corn with salt, the driver cranes his neck, visibly intrigued. The woman gets nervous, you have to pick quick, someone will report us for pedophilia. I choose the Orchid. The woman gives me the key through the opening in the booth. I say: Come on, Ana, and we go into the motel holding hands, our path lit by the headlights of the cars behind us.

16

I was having breakfast with Cora when the phone rang. It was Anthony, the executive producer of our channel in London. He said they were doing a show about epidemics and he'd learned that yellow fever was spiking again in Brazil, could I maybe shoot some images for them? I gave them the only answer I could and hung up. The request from London alerted me to an issue closer to home. I called Maju and asked if Cora had been vaccinated. She said she hadn't, she had tried at the local clinic and at the private hospital, but they were out of doses everywhere, she had already told me. I couldn't remember, I must have been focused on work or on Yara's curves. Why didn't you tell Cacá? Because he was in Rio, she said, and I got annoyed at my husband for his totemic laziness. He's lived in São Paulo for nearly twenty years and still hasn't bothered to find a doctor in town, having to go back to his hometown every time he has an ingrown toenail. And on top of that, we had a problem in that moment, because my editing brain was all up and running, and I couldn't stop organizing the scenes for a catastrophic trailer.

SCENE 1—HOUSE—EVENING

A mother arrives and finds her daughter lying on the couch. The girl is pale, sweating. Her mother checks her temperature. She looks alarmed at the thermometer.

SCENE 2—HOSPITAL—EVENING

The girl is lying on a stretcher, even more pale, looking

even more sickly. The doctor looks at her parents and shakes his head with sadness.

SCENE 3—CEMETERY—DAY

The girl lies inside a white coffin. People wait in line to see her. Her maternal grandmother cries, then comes close to the girl's mother, but instead of hugging her, she strikes the mother across the face. Her paternal grandmother does the same thing.

I learned from one of our documentaries that our brain doesn't distinguish between imagined and lived experience. Therefore, every mother has lived through the death of their child and the pain that follows, in nightmares and daydreams, for seconds, minutes, or even hours. What makes life bearable is the mix of good and bad projections we dream up, a kind of balance.

Still sitting at the table, I remembered a nursery rhyme popular with little kids. We heard it in a play when Cora was six months old, the stage filled with guitars, xylophones, and voices, the band playing to an audience of new mothers, all lifting up their babies to clap to the sound of lyrics, which went like:

There were ten of them kids.
One fell off his bike and broke his spine,
and then there were nine.
There were nine of them kids.
One ate cake, the cake was covered in mold,
and then there were eight.
There were eight of them kids.
One went on a riding lesson, the horse kicked him,
and then there were seven.
There were seven of them kids.
One went to see some flicks and there was a fire,

and then there were six.
There were six of them kids.
One got into a fight and got stabbed in the chest,
and then there were five.
There were five of them kids.
One went to war and never came back,
and then there were four.
There were four of them kids.
One got his degree and moved far away,
and then there were three.
There were three of them kids.
One ate a bad stew, the meat was rotten,
and then there were two.
There were two of them kids.
One wanted to have some fun, he got too drunk,
and then there was one.
There was only one kid.
He went out for a run and got lost,
and then there were none.

What a cheerful song, I thought at the time, looking around me and noticing the same discomfort in the other mothers, who were all checking for the emergency exits in the room in case of a fire, and clapping. Wow, yay, lots of clapping, because at this stage mothers believe even lack of enthusiasm can scar a kid.

Since that day, every time I got scared something might happen, I came up with stupid verses to help me unwind. That Friday, I said:

There were nine of them kids.
One didn't get her shots because her mother was too busy eating cake,
and then there were eight.

Then I called every clinic and hospital in town, and made my secretary do the same. But nothing, there wasn't a single dose anywhere, not even in Taubaté. I remembered the group chat from school. I told Cacá to ask about it there. He was helpful, as usual, and in five minutes we had our answer. The vaccine was indeed scarce, but one of the mothers found a Renault dealership in Santo André that offered vaccines to families who did a test drive.

I canceled all my morning appointments, shoved Cora and Maju in the back seat, and headed to the next town over. Cora was nervous, she was afraid of shots. Maju tried to calm her down, saying that she didn't have to be afraid, to trust God. I was jealous of her for believing in God like that, for having a crutch to help her get through life. Maybe that was the reason why I was never bothered by all the nonsense she told Cora. If it was good for the nanny, maybe it could be good for my daughter, and it's not like I had anything else to offer in my atheist simplicity. But then, suddenly, I became curious about what Cora thought. I asked: sweetie, what is God? The light was red, so I looked back and saw her thinking, her little finger on her chin, her eyes moving from side to side as if she were indeed looking for an answer in the deep drawers of her consciousness. God is love with a long beard, she finally said.

Then I left the two of them talking and went back to my world of short beards. I turned on the speaker phone to chase down a crew that could shoot the footage for Anthony. By the time we got to the dealership, I had already solved this and other problems, and was ready for our scene. I told Maju and Cora to follow my lead, and not go straight to the tent with the woman in a white coat and the sign: "fighting yellow fever." We would keep our dignity and get the dose by feigning genuine interest in the car. But as soon as we got near the door, Cora started to cry and scream: no shots. Since we couldn't deny it anymore, I decided to tell the salesperson that we'd been meaning to test drive a car for a while, and since my daughter needed the vaccine, I felt that was the perfect moment. I noticed his gaze on my bag, on the car keys I carried in my hand, on Maju behind me in her white uniform. As a good salesman, he must have seen the glimmer of possibility. He smiled and asked: what model? I pointed at one to my left.

We all got into the car. An unlikely quartet going down a glum street in Santo André, all because one day an arbovirus met a tropical mosquito called *Aedes aegypti*, which bit millions of people and created too much demand for a vaccine in a country with a strained healthcare system, scarce resources, and some mothers negligent enough to be the last to realize it. But there I was paying for my sins, hearing all about the motor, the sensors, something I actually found cool—headlights that sense when there's a car coming in the opposite direction and dim their beam. I think the salesman realized my listening was like that of a heroin addict waiting for a hit, because he didn't even bother driving very far. Soon he gave me directions to go back to the store, to Cora's disappointment, who was watching cartoons on the rear monitor. Even so, as we arrived, he brought me the chart with the financing options for the car and I deflected, saying I wanted to discuss the payment with my husband and would have to come back later. Meanwhile I started pushing Cora in the direction of the vaccination booth.

Just then, a woman came into the dealership. She caught my eye because of her modest appearance. Not only her clothes, she also had something in her demeanor—an embarrassment about being in the world I'd seen in some people, including Maju. She wore flip flops, her gray hair tied in a bun, and she carried her belongings in a plastic bag. In each hand, she held a boy—four- or five-year old identical twins. The dealership seemed short-staffed and the same salesman welcomed the woman. He looked at her the same way he looked at me, and already knew everything, just like I did. So much so he didn't even bother smiling, simply asking what she wanted. She wanted a test drive, she said. Do you have a driver's license? The woman went quiet. You can't test drive a car without a license. Can't I just see the car inside the store, then? she asked. You can, he said, but why do you want to see a car you'll never drive? The woman looked down, at her feet in flip flops. Then she raised her head: what can I do for them to get the vaccine? The vaccine is only for clients who do a test drive, those are the dealership's rules, he answered impatiently. Please, she said. I got the impression that if I hadn't been there, he'd have told them to get out right then and there. But I was, and the salesman looked at me, worried about my impression of him. Which wasn't positive, of course, so I gave him a stern look, the way I look at my employees when they mess up. He turned to the woman and said: I can make sure you get a vaccine, but just one, because otherwise there won't be enough for our clients. You have to choose which one of the boys you want to vaccinate. I was shocked by the solution that man had found, an alternative that managed to be even worse than the initial problem. And just like I wouldn't know what to do in such a situation, the woman also didn't. She looked at one of the boys, then at the other, her anxiety mounting, the bag's handles cutting into her hand. That was when I heard myself say: I'll take the car. I was bewildered by my reaction, the decision hadn't come out of my head, it had come from some other place, and with such strength I had to go along with it. Let's look at the numbers while they get vaccinated? I said, pointing at the boys and at Cora. Of course, the salesman said, and promptly went to tell the woman in the white coat that everyone was getting vaccinated, including the boys' grandmother.

Then he led me to a table and pulled up a chair for me. While he showed me the financing options, I wondered what on earth I was doing, what had gotten into me to impulsively buy a car. Maybe this would work for a millionaire or a reckless executive, but I was neither. There was still time to change my mind, but I didn't want to, and that conviction was what intrigued me the most. I'm no saint. I wasn't buying that car to save the twins and ease the so-called grandmother's anxiety. I was moved by their situation, of course, but it took something else to make me open my wallet. As I sipped lukewarm coffee at the dealership, I thought that I was buying that car because I needed it, because our car, which Cacá used the most, was more than ten years old and was looking beat-up. Also, it would be better to head out to my mother's farm with the Renault, so Cora wouldn't get on my nerves asking again and again: are we there yet? She would be distracted by the screen. This was the version my ego, always so creative, managed to come up with and I bought into it, and also bought the car, to be paid in ten installments, since I was still strapped for cash thanks to Varejão's painting. Only a few days later, as I handed the keys to Cacá, did I understand what had made me go through with the purchase: my guilt. That tyrant that from time to time occupied a throne in my mind, so cunning and devious to act without me even realizing. Recognizing the guilt was a good first step toward challenging and stripping that mad queen of her throne. Though by then it was too late; the car had been bought and Cacá was already gushing over whatever type of motor, and the brown leather seats that reminded him of his mother's couch. I admit that feeding my guilt gave me a certain pleasure. The queen made me hungry and also feasted in my contentment. It felt good to give Cacá that joy, and this pleasure also came from feeling that I was a good wife. A wonderful little wife. And as a reward, I was entitled to a little sidestepping with my lover.

But this all happened later. In that moment I was still blind as I filled out the forms, when the salesman asked if I didn't want to get a shot as well. I was going to say no, I don't know why I felt I was protected from everything. My blood must be cold or taste like Angostura bitters, because mosquitoes never bit me. It was actually humiliating how they refused to drink my blood even when I was the only person out on the balcony on a summer night. But it occurred to me that I could be going to Acre, and the mosquitoes there might not be as choosey as the ones spoiled by all the blood variety in the city. Playing the role of the cheater, it wouldn't look good to come home from an Amazonian hospital both with a fever and lovesickness. So I did, I got the vaccine. Maju and the boys' grandmother talked. In our society, equals attract. The two of them were already exchanging their mutual humilities. Maybe for the first time I noticed Maju looking at me with affection. The woman also looked at me the same way. She got up and kissed my hand. After that, she and the two boys left. The woman in the white coat pulled up my shirt sleeve and I got the shot, while my daughter still screamed because of hers.

I took Cora and Maju home along the canal, anxious to see what the crew had shot for Anthony. That's capitalism's clever little trap: once you scratch your itch and buy something, you reinforce the feeling of dependency on your job. In no time I was at the studio talking to the cameraman. He told me they'd shot the footage at the Cantareira mountain range. That was where the highest number of confirmed cases of yellow fever in the state were, about a hundred and sixty. More than people, *Aedes* had taken animals. Over seven hundred monkeys had already died from the disease in the area. The population started to believe the howler monkeys were to blame for the epidemic, because mosquitoes could contract the virus from an infected monkey and then pass it on to another monkey or person. But getting rid of the local monkeys was stupid, the cameraman explained. The transmitting vector was the one that should be eliminated, while the monkeys were victims too, and in a way our allies, because when they'd started dying, falling stiff off trees, they'd served as a warning that there were lots of mosquitoes in the area. But no one seems to understand this, he continued, and warned me about the grotesque scenes following.

He pressed play. At first, everything seemed fine. Monkeys calmly jumping from tree to tree, one of them in close-up eating a piece of fruit. Suddenly, a noise. Voices screaming unintelligible things. The camera shows a group of people approaching the woods, mostly women. One of them gets down and grabs a stone. You can see her pausing a moment, looking around, as if waiting for approval. It's a tense second, a narrative suspension; I hoped for the pregnant woman next to her to grab her hand, stop her from throwing that stone. But it's not what happens. The pregnant woman stretches out her arm like a general ordering to shoot. Feeling encouraged, the woman throws the stone toward the monkeys. By a stroke of luck, her aim is terrible. The stone hits a tree and falls, rolling on the ground. But war has been declared. Other people crouch down, grab pebbles, and throw them at the howler monkeys. The camera captures a hand with painted nails choosing the biggest stone, weighing it, then throwing it in slow motion. It's as if the cameraman had sniffed out the best scene, the flaccid body of a middle-aged mother externalizing her fear or maybe her frustrations in a single movement, the pain suddenly shaping her like an athlete, the knees flexed, her foot turned, her arm arched. The stone soars and squarely hits the head of a scared monkey trying to escape. The poor creature falls, blood flowing out of its head, through its nose. It was barbaric, said the cameraman. And I thought the same thing, until I realized I wasn't much different from those women. I too had started the day scared, willing to do anything to protect my child. The difference was that I'd been educated and informed. I had money to go into a car dealership, do a test drive that entitled me to a vaccine. Those mothers had been abandoned by the system. More primate than the monkeys themselves, since it's receiving and giving support that makes us human—though the term "human" made no sense in that moment.

The monkey ends up getting stoned to death, to the sound of screams I recognized as screams of justice. Isn't the footage incredible? the cameraman asked. I nodded, feeling what I'd felt so many times before, a mix of pleasure and sadness for being in possession of such shocking images.

17

I turn the Orchid's key. Before I even go in and see what's inside, I can already smell it. A mixture of mold and body odor and cleaning products—and cheap products at that, I can spot that fake lavender smell from a kilometer away. I take off Chickadee's shoes, her heels look pretty bad. Then I plug my phone to charge. Have I got any messages from Mr. Cacá and Mrs. Fernanda? Of course not, it's only eight o'clock, I see on the screen that's lit up. Two texts from Cacá. I'm about to read them but then stop myself, maybe it's best to pretend I didn't see them. I feel a bit guilty, sorry for Mr. Cacá, who's always so nice to me. But what's done is done, best to move forward. Especially because I have other stuff I need to do.

I type the Wi-Fi password I find on the nightstand, bigcorn69. I look for the Garcia bus company's phone number and call them. A man says there are no other buses today, but early tomorrow morning there's one going to Santa Cruz do Rio Pardo that drives through Presidente Prudente, one hundred and twenty reais for the ticket. I grab my bag, my card. Ana asks if she can watch TV and I say yes, while I read the numbers to the man, the expiration date, hoping we won't get disconnected in the middle of booking. It works. He says I'll receive an e-ticket over email and is about to hang up, but I ask him wait a moment, I want to see if I've really received it, I'm so scared of spending the money and getting stuck here. While I log into my email, I hear a strange sound, then lots of moaning. I turn around and see Ana sitting on the bed, Bibi on her lap, watching TV. On screen, there's an anus gaping open and so up close, it looks more like the crater of a volcano. What's that? Ana asks, pointing at the screen, at a big corn whose head is now rubbing against the folds. Where's the remote? I start screaming, the moaning starting over again. Our Lady of Aparecida, better the girl go blind than see something like this. I have to grab Cora to find the remote. The buttons are covered in a plastic sleeve, I have to press OFF twice to turn off that disgrace. As soon as the screen goes dark, Ana starts to cry. I want to watch cartoons, she says, her mouth gaping. I think of the other hole, did she realize that was an anus? Better not talk about it, maybe she'll forget. Then I remember I'm still on a call, the man is waiting, God, I'm so embarrassed, can he hear the TV? I don't have the nerve to talk to him again. I check if I received the email and hang up on the poor guy. Ana continues crying and repeating the same sentence—kids when they start begging for something, nothing can stop them. I decide to do what she wants, the poor thing doesn't have any toys, other than Bibi, she deserves to watch some cartoons. But of course I won't risk her seeing more porn. I tell her to go into the bathroom and close the door. She can only come out when Maju says so. I turn on the TV, quickly switch channels, find a news channel, then Shoptime selling gold-plated jewelry, and after that it's just black, nothing more. I wipe the phone on the nightstand with a towel. I call reception. A man answers. I ask if they don't have a cartoon channel. He's quiet. He seems to think it's a strange question, then says: what cartoon? Something like *Snow White and the Horny Dwarfs*? I'm so embarrassed I almost hang up again, but I'm paying to stay there, and paying well. I continue and say: cartoons for kids. The man says: this is a love motel, there's no kid stuff.

I tell Ana she can get out of the bathroom and explain there are no cartoons. She pouts. But before the screaming starts again, I have an idea. I get the receipt pad I took from the car wash and a pen and start doodling on the first page. Look, Ana, the flower Maju is drawing will appear on the other page too, I say, and show her the carbon copy. Ana is happy. I wish Neide was here to see how it was worth grabbing the pad. I hold Ana's hand and together we draw houses, clouds, a dog with its own little house. She asks me if I'm left-handed. I tell her that I am. She says it's sinister. I laugh. I leave Cora to draw alone and go take care of the rest. I grab a menu, and give it a look. Beef and fries, four-cheese pasta, Tarzan's sausage, meat in a bun. So dirty, I swear to God, I think, and laugh, remembering Mrs. Tarsila, who loved meat sandwiches, and maybe also big meat, that old lady had always been frisky. I ask Ana what she prefers, the meat or the pasta. I call the reception desk again and order the beef and fries with two plates, so we can share. Then I open the mini fridge, all rusty. They can make it a sale: buy a bottle of water get a tetanus infection.

I sit for a moment, then lie down on the bed. When will Mr. Cacá and Mrs. Fernanda call the police? By now we must already cross the border, but we're still here, only halfway. We will only reach Presidente tomorrow at lunchtime. I feel the bills in my bra, I'm scared of what I'm doing. I wish I had my book with me to help with the fear, that's why I've always liked reading, because there is not here. Soap operas also work for that, but who can keep up with a soap opera while working as a maid. In the first house where I worked, I may watch a bit of TV, but I had to sit on the floor. The boss had three daughters, all addicted to soaps, there was no room on the couch for me. At my second job, there was a TV in the maid's quarters, but there was no point, the cleaning woman who shared the room with me went to bed early and snored real loud. It was impossible to watch TV with all that noise. At my third job, I thought I finally can. Cibele—she didn't like to be called Mrs. or anything—she invited me to watch a soap opera with her on my first night. Sit with us, she said, pointing at an armchair next to her and her boyfriend. The next day, I showed up to see another episode but she didn't invite me to sit anymore. I walked around for a bit, acting like I was arranging the curtain, but she acted like she didn't see. Turned out, she was only nice to me when her boyfriend was there. He ended up dumping her, good for him. By then I had already given up on watching anything, I'd already gone to the books. It wasn't new to me, because I've always liked reading, since Mr. Miguel came by the farm selling books, but discovering Nora Roberts at a used bookstore near the bus station was a blessing. That woman only writes stuff I like. Neide wasn't into her books because she said it had too much love and not enough sex, but sex is to have not to read about. The characters make love, that she doesn't understand. The man doesn't lick her breasts, he owns them. He doesn't suck, he savors. He doesn't enter, he dives. He doesn't come, but completely gives himself over. And, in truth, the characters don't even make love, they're joined by their trembling flesh. It's another level. All this by the light of a fireplace or on top of crackling dry leaves. I'm not so stupid like men to pay to see people doing it like those two on the TV. In the book I left on the bus, Rosalind falls in love with an older man. It takes a while for them to go on a date. Before they finally do it, Rosalind is in front of the mirror, getting ready to go, and the ghost of an ancestor shows up and tears her shirt to pieces. From then on, every time she goes out with the gray fox, the spirit shows up and ruins her clothes. I told this to Neide and she made fun of the book, what a silly story. Not silly at all. How many times have I felt like Rosalind, ready to go out, all dressed up in front of the mirror, and then the cleaning lady I shared that room with showed up in my head, saying: you're so stupid, woman, and in that moment it also felt like my clothes fell to pieces. Lauro sometimes came to haunt me too. Every time I remember he left me without as much as a note, my face gets old, my cleavage looks like a sad hole.

And since I don't have anything to read and I haven't been keeping up with the soaps, I decide to switch to the news channel and to leave the TV on all night, what if there's some news of Cora's missing, like they had for Neide's baby. I knock on wood and put the remote on top of the TV, so there's no chance Chickadee can reach that high. Then I walk around the room a bit, I go to the bathroom to see if there are towels for the both of us, and a hair drier. Ana pokes me. Maju, look at the drawing I made for you. I crouch down. I like to look at her little face, at those teeth that will fall out soon, you know what this is? she asks. Of course I don't, what I see is a receipt with a wobbly circle and some strange lines inside. But I won't disappoint Ana, I'll at least try. A ball. A balloon. A pizza. A clown. A rocket ship. A planet. A brigadeiro. Cinderella's pumpkin. She laughs when I mention the pumpkin. No, silly Maju. It's a heart with you and I inside.

18

It was almost one in the morning when the plane landed. I'd never set foot in Acre before. The forest's smell, the heat that wouldn't lift up even at night made me feel like I was in another world. I grabbed my suitcase, fixed my hair in a mirror I found on the way, thinking where was my head to be going to a place like that, lying to my boss, to my husband, saying I had to supervise a shoot we were already done filming.

Soon I found out my head was between my legs. So much so I felt a twinge in my pelvis when I saw Yara waiting for me, leaning against a dirty truck that must have belonged to the production. I got in, we kissed. Where are we going? I asked as soon as I managed to compose myself. Until that moment, Yara had given me no details about the trip and I didn't want to ask too many questions. We're going to Tarauacá, about three hours from here, and then to São Vicente, where we'll take the boat at six in the morning to go up the river to the village. Won't you get tired from driving all night? I'm a director, I'm used to all nighters. She put her hand on my thigh and warned me: you better get ready, cause in two hours we'll lose signal. And then, all communication. There isn't even a phone in the village. Not even a pay phone? She shook her head. I panicked, thinking about Matthew, Cacá, Cora, and the frightening possibility of being bitten by a snake without even being able to call an ambulance.

Already considering what I'd tell my boss, I asked her about the shoot. Yara said it was excellent, even the otter had followed the schedule; she described a few scenes. I left Matthew a message saying the exact opposite, that the shoot was a disaster, that we might need to go with a different animal, so much so I'd made the sacrifice of going in person to the Amazon. Then I left Cacá a message, then Cora, then my assistant, who knew what I was up to and would cover for me, if necessary.

I would have continued fiddling with my phone if Yara hadn't lit a joint, turned on the radio, and started singing the chorus of a country song with the weird "r." I copied her, we laughed. What an unjust world, I thought. If Cacá were the one singing and smoking weed on a bumpy road like this one, I'd have grabbed the joint off his hand, turned off the radio, and told him to watch the road, but lovers are lovers. So I simply changed the subject, and asked how she knew the Yaminawás.

Yara told me she'd first been in the Sete Estrelas village when she was nine. Her mother was researching Amazon tribes. They stayed for two months, and during that time she befriended a Yaminawá girl her age, Shakuna. Seven years later, when Yara was sixteen and her mom had already disappeared, her father said he wanted to go back to Sete Estrelas to research alligators. She suspected he didn't really have any reason to be there, just wanted to check if that's where she was. She wasn't; but going there ended up being nice, among other things because Yara and Shakuna reunited and rekindled their friendship. A few years ago, Shakuna had visited Yara in the States with her husband. The Yaminawá woman was going to an Amerindian conference, she had become a prominent figure. She was the first woman *pagé* of her ethnicity. How did she do it? I asked with genuine interest, but can't remember Yara's answer—I was already heavy with sleep, my eyelids trying to end the shift we'd started at six that morning. She looked at me and said that's what happens when you enter the unplugged world, the body relaxes. Then she took a hand off the wheel and touched me. I fell asleep.

I think it was the rocking of the car that woke me. Or the sunlight announcing another day, hitting the houses on the only street of São Vicente. Everything in the village existed around the Gregório river, that was how the boats came up to the villages. We parked by the water, and Yara fully woke me up with a morning-breath kiss. We got out, and she unloaded our bags. I noticed she'd brought a gallon of water, bread, and high-fiber cookies. You might not like the food at the village, she told me, and I felt for her the love we can only feel for people who take care of us.

I looked at my phone, even the clock wasn't synced, a sign we really were in another dimension. An indigenous man who was also waiting for a boat told us it was six fifteen. Did we miss it? I asked Yara. She laughed. Of course not, our boat leaves at six o'clock local time, which really means whenever they feel like it. It might be at six thirty, seven, even eight. Never at six fifteen. It was true, there was no sign of the boat for a while, only mosquitoes, making me ever more scared of getting malaria. I covered myself with bug repellent up to the inside of my ears. Take this, Yara said, handing me a vitamin B supplement, which, according to her, would make my blood even more unpalatable than it already was.

At around seven, our boat arrived. Actually, it was a motorized canoe, with wood planks for seats. We loaded our luggage. I wanted to sit next to her, but the boatman didn't let me, we had to sit on opposite ends to balance out our weight. We started our four-hour journey upstream, which seemed absurd at first but eventually made sense. As Yara said, it takes time to venture beyond the reach of Starbucks. The further we moved away from capitalism, the more the world around us blossomed with beauty.

Finally, we arrived at the bottom of a hill. From down there, we couldn't see anything. I got up expecting to find stairs. As I stepped onto the shore, I was pleasantly surprised by a big field surrounded by traditional *ocas*, children running in straw skirts, some women with bare breasts, and voices singing. A woman, who I assumed was Shakuna, came to us. She hugged Yara, then me. We went to her house. I thought it would be a bigger *oca*, more private, wasn't she a *pajé*? But her dwelling was just like everyone else's, with bamboos and hammocks hanging inside, and a big table in the kitchen. You must be starving, she said, and asked her sister-in-law to serve lunch.

While we ate, Shakuna said it was best to have a light dinner, it wasn't good to take uni on a full stomach. Uni? I asked. The people singing outside, Shakuna said, and paused so I could hear the distant singing. They're preparing the uni. Yara turned to me and said: it's what they call ayahuasca. I must have widened my eyes because she said I didn't have to take it if I didn't want to. Or you can try just a little bit, Shakuna suggested. But then you can't have sex for a whole day, she continued, looking at us with a maternal smile. I tensed up. I was fine with drugs, but only the ones approved by the FDA or investigated by the FBI. I tried to change the subject and asked Shakuna how she'd managed to become a *pajé*. She said it was difficult, she'd had to stay isolated in the forest for nine months to prove she was as strong as a man. And during that entire time she survived on very little food, only what she could hunt and the uni, which she took every day in order to talk to the spirits. I think Shakuna could sense my shock, because she explained that in her community it was normal to spend some time alone in the woods to gain strength.

Then she and Yara caught up on what had happened in each other's lives in the past few years, until Shakuna showed us to our *oca*. It was away from the village—according to the *pajé*, tourists enjoy privacy—in a clearing in the middle of the forest, near a stream. The *oca* stood on stilts and had a pretty straw roof but no walls. Nor a bathroom. As soon as Shakuna left, I asked: are we going to sleep here? We are, Yara said, and started to hang our hammocks. We put on our swimsuits, grabbed our toiletry bags, and walked toward the stream, in the company of an impressive number of butterflies. Out of nowhere, Yara stopped. Look, what a beautiful *Scolopendra.* I looked down and saw a repulsive centipede crawling in front of us. I had the urge to squash that thing, but stayed still, hearing Yara say: look at those colors, look at its antennas. She continued staring at the arthropod for a while. I even thought she might be high, but then realized I hadn't seen her smoke. When the centipede disappeared in the bushes, we went on. And then it was my turn to be impressed, seeing the landscape in its totality. A crystalline creek cut through the forest, branches and flowers bowing to the water as if in reverence. On the side we were on, there was a thin sandy strip. A private beach. It was almost 90 degrees, it was wonderful to jump in the water. Yara wedged the bottle of soap between two rocks, and started scrubbing my hair. She washed my head, my face, my shoulders. She untied my bikini top and put her foamy hands on my nipples. I did the same for her, our bikinis floating beside us. Then we dove together. We swam to the sandbank and lay in the shallow, with just enough water to cover our bodies, and did hoka-hoka.

When we looked around, we realized our tops had disappeared downstream, which wasn't that big of a problem in that place. We lay on the sand, our four nipples staring at the sun. Yara lit a joint. We talked for a long time. At one point, we heard a noise. I looked around and saw a sort of pig, but tiny, not far from me. Yara said not to be scared, it was just a harmless *caitiu.* Then she lay back down on her elbows, her gaze distant, toward the creek's bend. When I was little, I had a recurring nightmare, she said. I dreamed the city lights took over the countryside, like a plague. They even popped up in the valley behind the ranch where we lived. Then, facing me: sometimes I think it's turned out to be real. You know what percentage of mammals are wild? 20? I guessed. Four percent. The rest are humans and their pets. We've meddled with nature so much there's a biologist who says the period we're living in shouldn't even be called the Anthropocene. It should be called the Eromocene. What does that mean? The era of loneliness. I moved closer, kissing the sadness in her mouth. Then we walked in silence to the *oca*, maybe because we were tired or in peace. Or both. Yara lay in a hammock, saying she'd take a nap. I lay in the other, thinking I wouldn't be able to fall asleep, but five minutes later I was out.

We woke up to the sound of plates clinking. Shakuna sent you these tapiocas, a boy said, also leaving two glasses of juice. As the sun went down, Yara lit up an oil lamp. We were still sluggish. We ate in silence on the edge of the stilt structure, our legs touching from time to time. Then we brushed our teeth with water from the bottle she'd brought and we walked with our lamps to the center of the village.

I noticed lots of people were climbing up the hill that led to Sete Estrelas. Yara explained they were Yaminawás from neighboring villages. On Saturday night everyone got together for the ceremony, which I guessed would be taking place in the field, where there now was a bonfire. In the back, there was a long table with two chairs and two stout jars, their openings covered with fabric. Shakuna suddenly appeared with a bead serpent around her neck. She greeted us with the same warmth and asked how we were doing. Then she introduced us to lots of people, including another *pajé* who would be guiding the ceremony with her. He wanted to know if this would be my first time, referring to the ayahuasca. I didn't know what to say, I wasn't even sure I was going to take that stuff. I was shitting myself from the fear of something happening in the middle of the forest. On the other hand, I didn't want to waste the chance to try it in a place like that, with Yara. I said I would. Yara smiled. Soon after, she pulled me over to the table, where Shakuna and the other *pajé* now sat, a line in front of each one.

When it was our turn, Shakuna said she'd just give me a little to start. If I felt nauseous, I could throw up in the bushes. And look for her if necessary. Then she handed me a cup with two fingers of uni. I looked around and saw Yara downing a full cup. I downed mine. We sat down together by the fire. Soon I started to feel this weight in my stomach, some unexpected burps. What I wanted the most was to steal a kiss from Yara, but the gas wasn't helping. Even if I were to kiss her, she was already somewhere else, her eyes closed, swaying to the music. I closed my eyes too, hoping to feel the effects of that twig soup, but more time went by and nothing. I watched people, listened to the melody. I noticed how simple the lyrics were, free of any metaphors or narrative, maybe to give more room to the subconscious, like a trampoline that only exists to aid the jump. About half an hour later, I noticed Yara was crying. I wiped her tears. Her eyes looked different, or maybe I was the one who was seeing better now. In her pupils, dilated by the night and the tea, I saw a sadness beyond that caused by the loss of wildlife or nature. Yara had a sadness of someone who has no place to go back to. I hugged her. I asked how she was. She said fine, it was good to cry. And you, are you feeling anything? I said no. She grabbed my hand and said: come on.

The line was starting to form again, with the same people, suggesting it was normal to have a second round. We went in together. Shakuna asked if I was all right. I said I was. She gave me a full cup. The *pajé* gave Yara another. We drank. This time I wanted to feel it, to understand what everyone was feeling—later I learned the trip is always unpredictable, never repeats itself. I also learned the amount you take doesn't guarantee anything, but that being relaxed really helps. And help it did, because this time the uni hit me hard. I started to feel strong waves of nausea. Just throw up, Yara said, it'll be good for you. She brought me to the edge of the field, where other people were also puking their guts out. From afar, I saw the *pajé* watching me and realized how small-minded I was, thinking of being alone and helpless in that place, when I was supported by a community and wisdom spanning hundreds of generations. Their knowledge recommended taking uni with a purpose—it's not by chance they called it "medicine." I thought about Yara, about what I'd do with my marriage if things went in the direction I thought they might be going. But as someone later told me, you can ask for an answer or the cure to something, and you might even get it, but the tea decides what needs to be healed. And the tea showed me Cora. With my eyes shut, I saw my daughter ten times her size, standing in front of a tiny door she tried to open but couldn't. She turned the doorknob, looked into the keyhole, pushed it, and nothing. Then, just as it had appeared to me out of nowhere, the image suddenly vanished. In its place, I saw myself in the house where I grew up. I wandered around the rooms, saw details I didn't remember, that must have been stored in an inaccessible part of my memory and now sprouted out with the same palpable quality of a dream: me opening my father's cigar case on the coffee table, seeing the red Menendez label. I knew I was in my child body because in a moment I saw myself in the garden, with the overalls I wore when I was five years old. I fearfully looked at the tall plants my parents never pruned and the trash they let accumulate in that gloomy backyard. I called out for my mother several times, but no one came for me. Until I reappeared as an adult and took my child self in my arms. It's O.K., I said, we'll leave this place. I felt we should look for someone else, but in that moment I opened my eyes and it all stopped.

How much time had passed? The fire was still burning, but the indigenous people and Yara were on the other side of the field, singing in a circle, holding hands, their silhouettes and voices elongated by the moon. I touched Yara's shoulder, and came between her and an older woman, at first feeling somewhat ridiculous, singing in a circle like a child, but soon realizing the problem wasn't the singing but judging it. Judging everything, all the time. Taken by the music, I started to feel the barrier between myself and the other people and the plants and the moon disintegrate. And being everything, I wasn't me anymore. And not being me, I didn't suffer as much. It was the closest to the divine I'd ever been, something no religion with its liturgical effort had offered me. Later, Yara told me the Church had always tried to ban ayahuasca for this reason, because it realized its power. While Catholics and Protestants needed an intermediary—the priest, the bishop—to reach God, the tea dismantled that hierarchy, putting anyone in direct contact with the divine or something that feels like it.

By then, the indigenous people had started to form a line for the third round and Yara asked if I wanted more. I said no, I was feeling so good I didn't want to ruin it. She said she didn't want it either. We stayed there for a while, watching the circle dissolve, the drums returning, until she said: wanna go? We walked back to our *oca*. As I looked up from the path lit by the lantern, I saw the sky already lighting up; we could make out the outline of our hut. Yara jumped onto the structure and reached out her hand to help me on. She asked if I was hungry. I said no, but she insisted we should eat. We shared a fruit and shared the visions we'd had with the uni. Then I put on my nightgown, and she put on a t-shirt, that mutual look of lust. We started to kiss. Remember we can't? I said. And she said: I'll kill Shakuna.

Resigned, we lay in our hammocks, listening to the animals, to the creaking of the hammock, until a hand crawled like a spider into my mosquito net, pulling up the tulle. I felt Yara's body nestling against mine, the hammock swaying to accommodate the bigger load. We can't, she whispered, and squeezed my nipple. We can't, I repeated, and pulled up my nightgown. We continued moving closer and closer saying "we can't," until our mouths touched, and our nipples, our pussies, and we fucked our mirrored images in the hammock. When we were finished, we didn't move or turn around, there was no room for that. And if there was, I didn't want to. Looking into her dilated pupils, I said: I love you. I love you too, she said, looking into mine.

We woke up with the sun high up like an overhead lamp. We took a quick swim and went to lunch carrying our luggage; soon it would be time to leave. Shakuna welcomed us to the table, as her sister-in-law took a fish from the grill. We ate. Yara took some pictures.

Then the *pajé* walked us to the river, where a boatman who couldn't have been more than sixteen was waiting for us, one foot on the ground, the other on the hull. I said goodbye and went aboard. Shakuna and Yara continued talking a bit—I think Shakuna mentioned the possibility of meeting soon, I'm not sure, because I ended up getting distracted by the boatman, by the scars on his stomach. He had dozens of little white dots on his skin, scars like the ones I'd seen in a documentary, from wounds opened to apply frog venom. I only remembered it because I'd been intrigued. How good must the high from it be, for indigenous people to hurt themselves like that? I decided to ask the boatman. He confirmed the scars were indeed from applying the venom and said it was a horrible feeling, a nightmare. How many times have you taken it? Fifteen, I started when I was seven, he said with pride, showing me three round scars on his ribs. After we left, I realized the purpose of taking the venom. Besides purifying the body, it was a way to gain courage, which is why he was so proud of showing off his scars. Doing kambo and ayahuasca isn't exactly pleasant; neither is spending months alone in the forest like Shakuna and the others. This seemed strange to me, because in our society the only thing that makes sense is pleasure. But indigenous people's focus had nothing to do with hedonism. They trained to face their fears. Everything is a means to learning to get past them, which I found fascinating, having been taught to suppress them. Be brave, don't be afraid, I heard all my life. And I wondered: can someone not be afraid? Of course not, hence the feeling of impotence I experienced, because fear keeps coming back. I thought that from that moment on I would tell Cora: go despite the fear. If I had waited for mine to disappear, I wouldn't have lied to Cacá and Matthew, wouldn't have boarded that plane, wouldn't have gone to the malaria endemic area, wouldn't have traveled up a river with no phone service or hospitals, wouldn't have taken ayahuasca, wouldn't have seen a forest that might not even exist in twenty years, wouldn't have heard "I love you" in a hammock. With that satisfaction and my hair disheveled by the wind a few hours later I arrived in São Vicente.

It was almost evening and we still had a long way ahead. Which wasn't a problem, I'd travel to the North Pole with that woman. But I had a flight, a life, all that. We loaded the truck, got ready to leave, but before that Yara said she needed a Coke. I found it unusual, I had never seen her drink one, why this sudden need? We went into the only local store, which sold everything from potatoes to dresses. Leaning against the counter, Yara opened the can and offered me some. I told her I didn't really like Coke. She said she didn't either, but it was something she did with her mom and dad. Every time they came back from a fieldwork in the middle of nowhere, they had a Coke. Not for the taste, but to tell their body: we're back.

Then we hit the road, time flying by. I didn't even realize service was back and I could turn on my phone. It seemed so serious to be out of reach like that, but forty-eight hours and almost two hundred messages later, nothing important had happened. At one point we talked about the future, which made me happy—only someone in love makes plans. Of course, it was a near future, Yara had no clue where she'd be in a year, but after our series, she'd be heading to Scotland to shoot the migration of a pack of wolves. With much satisfaction, she told me the Scots had realized they needed wild animals to balance out the ecosystem, so they decided to import a wolf pack from Denmark. It's going to be so beautiful to see them arrive, she said, and squeezed the wheel. And then: I could rent a house on a hill. We can savor the beautiful view. I don't know what surprised me more, the verb "savor" or the invitation. I said I couldn't disappear for a month, I had a daughter, a husband, a job. She said I should bring Cora too, she'd help me take care of her. As for work, I could do it remotely. And to the husband, I could just say I'd met the love of my life. Though I thought she might just have been joking, I felt cold and warm at once. I said I'd think about it. And I really would. During the next few days, I thought about it every waking moment, about getting to know Yara in a world so different from mine. Maybe this is why passion is so powerful, because it's also about a passion for a new possibility for oneself.

19

The motel phone rings. I jump, how can they find us here? I think don't answer, but that can be even worse, if the reception people or whoever it is will come here in person. I pick up and say: hello. The plate is in the drawer. I say: O.K., and hang up, and only then realize how strange what he just said. I'm not ignorant, I've stayed in many hotels with my bosses before, and they're all the same, someone rings the bell, comes into the room, and leaves a tray on the table with a plate on top. I've always loved it, it's so fancy. But food in the drawer, what on earth is this? I call the reception desk. The man tells me to look at the wall, there is a big gray drawer. Here it is, a metal square with a pull, I actually thought it was a light box. I open it and find the beef with fries.

I put the plate on the table. It's so small it's like an ironing board with two chairs. The food is also pretty small, I don't understand this thing of using lettuce as a bed, maybe it's to distract from the ugliness of the beef full of nerves, I have to cut it into tiny pieces so Ana can chew. Then I sit down, eat my dinner too. Not even two minutes later I rehear a sound, a door slamming, a woman's voice saying: come quick because I like to fuck crying. Just what we needed. I get up and raise the volume on the TV to cover the noise from next door. Ana complains, it's too loud, but soon we get distracted with a game I make up. She says I am hungry and I say yes, I ate for three. She says: can I get a toothpick, and I say, I don't have a brick, and so it goes, I pretend I can't hear well and she crying from laughter.

When we're done with dinner, I lower the volume on the TV, and tell her it's bath time. I go to the sink, grab a bottle of shampoo and one of soap, tiny bottles with an apple on the label, Forbidden Fruit Love Motel. Big Corn's man can't even make his own products. I turn on the faucet. It gets warm quickly, but so little water, just some drops. It's no problem for me, but can you imagine washing a child's head at this pace? It's going to take more than five minute just to rinse the shampoo, with her screaming—which is kind of normal in a love motel, but not a child in a love motel—and the last thing I want is to call attention to ourselves. I think of not washing her hair, but I can't find a shower cap, what can I do? I look at the bathtub. The millions of germs in there look back at me. My face gets red just from thinking about where they've been. I must disinfect it.

I remember what I saw on the mini-bar. I go there, look at the Old Eight label, forty percent alcohol. Seagers, forty-five percent, even better, but it must be gin from Paraguay, you can't really believe what's on the label. I check the price on the menu. Paraguayan for sure, I just don't know if to save money they put more or less alcohol in the bottle. I take a quick swig. It must be very concentrated, because it burns my stomach. With the bottle open, I run back to the bathroom, Chickadee after me, curious to see what I do. I pour the gin in the bathtub, but it's too little, not enough to cover the whole tub and I don't want to use another bottle, the Old Eight costs an arm and a leg. I have an idea, a way of killing the bacteria for good. I go to my purse and dig inside. I find what I need, a matchbox from a restaurant where I had dinner with Mrs. Fernanda. I strike the red head and throw it in the bathtub. A huge flame comes on. Ana cheers, she clapping next to me. I turn on the water quick, now the fire must go away, but nothing comes out of the faucet, it only makes a noise and not even a drop. The flame spreads. Our Lady of Aparecida, now I'm going to burn down this motel, I never imagined this is how they find us, on national television burning to a crisp on a roadside motel. I run to grab a glass, fill it with water, but then the bathtub faucet pours out, a stinky squirt that puts out the fire and all the panic inside me. I sit next to the bathtub and start laughing. Ana laughs with me, that was so cool, Maju. Then, when I wipe the tears from so much laughing, she says: I love you. What did you say, Chickadee? I love you.

It isn't the first time she says that, but maybe it's the first time I'll answer. I wasn't taught to say this. I know that my nana Brígida loved me because she did everything for me, but I never heard the sentence come out of her mouth, no one at the farm said it, it was like love was something too delicate for us, a box of bonbons with pretty paper that only some hands may unwrap. We lived together for fifteen years, slept in the same bed, we felt so much love for one another and we never said it, not even on her deathbed. Then for years I didn't say it because I didn't feel it, love seemed like a privilege, a stroke of luck you can show off, like those couples kissing in the street. Then Lauro came along and I found out I love too, but saying it was a different story. After two months together he said I love you and I nearly died, I looked at him stiff like an ear of corn, what do I do now? A fear of giving him that phrase I never gave even to my grandmother. And a fear of spending something that I'd learned only happens one time. So I didn't say it, the phrase stopped behind my teeth, I got stuck with the I love you inside my mouth, wondering do I get it out or not? until I finally answered him, quietly and stuttering, eight days later. I'm not the only one, I know I'm not. Maids know people's lives behind closed doors, we know their underwear from the inside out, so I know saying I love you isn't for everyone. Some men go their whole lives without saying it to a son. Some women go their whole lives without saying it to their husbands. And there are people like Neide who say it to everybody. I thought it was bad when I met her, a slutty thing to do, to say it to just about anyone. Until I started to notice how happy Neide was, how happy Lauro was, and that maybe they were happy because they loved more, and maybe they loved more because they said I love you. As someone told me once, hunger will come when you eat. Maybe love comes when you love. I learned and started saying it, only occasionally and to the right people as is my way, and I wanted to say it back to Cora when she said it to me at Mrs. Fernanda's home—when she jumped out of bed in the middle of the night to sleep next to me in my little room—I only didn't say it because it was reckless of me to say it to a boss's daughter. But now she's mine. I say: I love you too. She doesn't care, she's already distracted doing something else. She's leaning over the bathtub, trying to touch the water with the tip of her fingers. Get your hand out, Ana. I filled it up to let it stew and rinse off the dirty, I'll fill it again in a bit. I get down to open the drain. The water goes down, it gets less and less. Ana looks at it, maybe she will even like the bath. I turn around to get the soap. She calls me. Look, Maju. She points at the drain, at the water spinning quickly. The water is a ballerina, she says, smiling at me.

20

After I got back from the Amazon, I met up with Yara a few times. Then she went to Espírito Santo to shoot another episode for the series, and the silence started. I texted her for a few days and nothing. I didn't overthink it. The crew's job was precisely to get away from technology, I'd be concerned if they were filming jaguars by a pay phone. But after nearly a week I started to get worried. Had she met someone else? Had an Ocelot eaten her? I asked Agnes to discreetly check. She soon informed me my director had landed in São Paulo the day before, at 10 A.M. I was surprised, if she was in the same city as me, why hadn't she reached out?

I left work and stopped home to take a shower. Excluding the scenarios ending at the morgue, I hoped our encounter would lead to some action. When I got home, Maju welcomed me without her white uniform. Good thing you're here, I wanted to text you, I thought you forgot the party. Of course I had forgotten, but I quickly remembered. The birthday girl's mother had sent a *save the date* to all the school moms two months before the big day, as if someone would postpone a trip or even a doctor's appointment because of her event. Maju said she'd texted me saying she couldn't go to the party because she had her conjugal visit. And I had said it was fine. I really had, though I hadn't realized that the person who had to go with Cora to the party—she was already there, the whole class went straight from school—would be me, as my husband was delivering a cactus to a wedding.

Out of options, I grabbed my purse and went to fulfill my duty. I rang the doorbell at number 25 Clélia Street. A woman in uniform opened the door and only then did I realize I didn't know what the birthday-girl's mother looked like. While I walked around the yard, at the back of the house, I looked through my planner, but couldn't find her name or phone, let alone a picture. I greeted the mothers, all sitting at a table with the same enthusiasm. Then I went after Cora, who was getting her face painted by a woman in a clown costume. I saw her eyes light up with joy when she saw me. I kissed my daughter, said hello to her friends. I asked Cora who the birthday-girl's mother was. She pointed at a redhead. Then she ran after the other girls.

I pulled up a chair and joined the moms. I only knew one of them—the mother of a girl who somctimcs came over to our place—but still we weren't close. The others I had only seen around, having waved or raised my eyebrows at them at school events. At any rate, it wasn't worth striking up a side conversation. There were only seven or eight of us, I'm not sure; the others watching the kids were nannies, sitting in the corners of the garden. I sat there sipping my beer and listening to the conversation. One of the moms, who had under-eye bags down to her ankles, said that since her son was born she hadn't known what sex was. Another one, who was wearing a mini skirt, said for her it was the opposite, she was having more sex than ever—though she didn't specify with whom. This second woman was the mother of my daughter's friend. I'd seen her around the neighborhood before the girls were born. I realized that since becoming a mother, Renata had indeed changed: she was sexier, as if marking her territory with her mini skirts, the small fabric indicating that her body was still the same homeland it had always been, motherhood hadn't destroyed her. Having a child was a strong punch that sent each of us to the corner of the ring, stars spinning around our heads. Not knowing who we were anymore, we slipped into extremes. We either lost our sexual identity or our desire came back stronger. We either dove into work or didn't know what to do with our lives, leaving our careers to try new things or falling into existential crises that could last for years. We were so insecure in our role as mothers that we needed to put down our peers. In that moment, I was witnessing all of us in the common practice of commenting on the questionable or regrettable choices of other mothers. So and so lets her son sleep in their bed. So and so spoils that girl with everything she wants. Another one left the baby with her grandmother for twenty days. It's unusual to see people questioning others' behavior to this extent, at least not for such petty reasons. Undermining other mothers helps lessen the constant feeling that we're doing a terrible job. I'm no exception. I share the same weaknesses, with the added compulsion of increasingly checking my phone. The checkmarks indicated that Yara had read my texts. What do you mean she's read my messages? So far, they'd appeared as unread, which reassured me; she could have lost her phone. But in that moment I knew it: she didn't want to talk to me.

I tried to get back into the conversation, but my mind was somewhere else. I apologized to the redhead, but I needed to leave before they sang "Happy Birthday." She whispered that the girl's mother was somebody else and pointed at her. Five minutes later I left the party with Cora kicking and screaming that she didn't want to leave before the cake, as I stuffed brigadier in her mouth. I started driving home. With Cora up, there wasn't much I could do. But suddenly, silence. Cora had cried herself to sleep and nothing would wake her up now. I thought, why not go? My daughter was so tired there was no chance of her waking up. I shoved my pride somewhere between the hand break and my seat and pressed the gas pedal, now to Yara's.

I quickly rang the doorbell, my hand immediately going back to hold Cora. Yara looked at me through the window. I smiled at her, and she smiled back with discomfort. She came out of the house, walked hesitantly to the gate, and greeted me with a kiss too dry for her standards. Is that Cora? she asked, pulling the hair off my daughter's face and looking at her with tenderness. Then she tensed up again. Did something happen for you to come all the way here? I was worried cause you haven't text me back, I said. I moved toward the door, rushed by my daughter's weight.

We went in. I only didn't drop Cora for fear of breaking her. There was a woman in the living room, sitting very comfortably, wearing simple clothes and barefoot. This is Violeta, Yara introduced her. The woman got up and smiled at me. I settled Cora on the couch. Then I kissed my new acquaintance on the cheek, she smelled of shampoo. I sat down with the two of them and only then could I finally take in the whole picture. She was about seventy, white hair in a bob. She wasn't exactly beautiful but very elegant. An elegance I couldn't place, since she wore no accessories or makeup. It was something that came from within, in the way she held her wine glass, in how she smiled. Why did she smile so much? Yara told me they were old friends, from Corumbá. Violeta was staying at her house while she was in São Paulo for her book launch. She's a poet, and it was that word, "poet," that made Violeta smile again, clearly happy with herself. An explanation had been offered; they were old friends. Could she have dated Yara's father? Of course there were the unanswered messages, that she yet had to explain, but maybe she hadn't had the chance. So, there was nothing to worry about. I even accepted a glass of wine. I started to drink in a pleasant state of relaxation, while I listened to Yara talk about how the shoot in Espírito Santo had been wonderful, perhaps becoming the best episode in the series. After asking Yara a question about the footage, I started to talk with Violeta. I think I asked her where the launch would be because she mentioned a small bookstore, explaining that essentially no one reads poetry. She then told me that once, at another book launch, only one person had showed up. Violeta had signed the book, taken a picture, talked for a while. Moved by the situation, the spectator bought a copy to support her. But that was in the beginning of your career, before you won the Jabuti Prize, Yara said. I noticed a hint of pride for her friend. That's true, before the prize, Violeta admitted modestly, lowering her gaze to her wine glass. Then she invited me to her book launch and poured me more wine, saying I had barely savored it. I had heard the word "savor" from Yara before. So, was it from Violeta that all that vocabulary, too sophisticated for a foreigner,—or even for a Brazilian—came from?

When Yara went to the restroom, I took my chance. I told Violeta I needed to go too and would use the bathroom upstairs. I don't think she heard me, she seemed not to hear anything below screaming. I went upstairs and walked into the bedroom. I found the bed unmade, with two pillows. Next to the mattress, a poetry book, a vitamin bottle, and reading glasses. In the bathroom, I saw a second toothbrush and a pair of underwear too big to be Yara's hanging from the shower. I looked at myself in the mirror, saw my eyes tearing up. I took a deep breath, fixed my hair. I went downstairs with a smile, pretending everything was fine, but without even realizing, I started provoking them with my sarcasm. And for that kind of thing, Violeta had great ears. After my second or third snarky comment, she said she was going to the corner store to buy cigarettes.

As soon as the door shut, I asked Yara if she was fucking Violeta. She said she wasn't, they'd dated many years ago, when she lived in Corumbá. Since then, they hadn't been involved. They were friends. So much so Violeta had been kind enough to leave us alone to talk, claiming she had to buy cigarettes when she didn't even smoke. I said if that was the case, why was she avoiding me. She said she knew I wouldn't take this situation very well. And also she couldn't deny her friend a place to stay. As soon as Violeta left, she would have reached out to me. Then she refilled our glasses, and moved closer to me. But if one day I slept with someone else, what would be the problem? I was speechless. It took me a moment to answer: what do you mean, what would be the problem? You said you loved me. I really do love you, I want to be with you, but I'm not naive enough to think we're never going to sleep with anyone else ever again. What a blow. Such brutal honesty about the fragile physiology of monogamy. What was I supposed to say? That at least in the beginning I need to believe we're going to have our hymens joined forever? Maybe I could have said that, but in that moment the door creaked and Violeta came in. With no cigarettes, eating a cheese bun. The moon is pregnant, she said, making me wonder how Yara could bear that factory of poetic suppositories all day. Her Portuguese must not have been very good. Or maybe she needed a mother at the time, who's to say. But the truth is that, lyricisms aside, Violeta seemed like a nice person. Maybe even interesting. She called us out to the garden to see the moon, which was a good idea. She talked about the stars, and a recent discovery that put in question the astronomic principles that had originated astrology. We chatted a bit about the subject, laughing at the thought of a hardcore Aquarius having an astrological identity crisis upon realizing they might actually be a Pisces.

Then we went back to the living room; Yara wanted to smoke. They sat next to each other on the couch and started to roll the joint as if in an assembly line. One grinding the weed, the other making the filter. One rolling the joint, the other flicking the lighter. As if their sync wasn't enough, they started talking about a friend of Yara's father, a certain Roundup—a man so unpleasant he got that pesticide nickname—and they remembered a scandal he once caused, which sent them into fits of laughter. To the point of tears, to the point of slapping each other's thighs. And all this before they'd even took a puff.

They might not have anything going on now, but watching that enviable chemistry all night would be agonizing. I thought it best to spare myself. I said I needed to go home. Yara told me to wait and smoke with them. I said I was driving and had Cora with me. It wasn't a good idea to be drunk and stoned at the wheel. I kissed them on the cheek, picked up my daughter, and walked out.

Yara followed me outside and helped me put Cora in the car. She said I should come to the book launch. There would be lots of cool people, friends of hers and Violeta's from Mato Grosso do Sul who were now living in São Paulo. I didn't reply, just said goodbye and took off. Later, like any person tormented by love and therefore by cyclical obsessive thoughts, I started to think I might have overreacted, and then that I hadn't, then that I had, then that I hadn't, then that I had . . . And so on, until I clung to the option that would give me an excuse to talk to her.

I got home and dropped my daughter on her bed with her clothes still on. Then I went to the living room and, staring at the blood-stained tiles, I sent her a voice message: I left in a hurry and forgot to say I love you. In that exact moment, Cacá came in, his tie loose, carrying a cactus and a succulent.

21

Finally, bath time. I check the temperature, not hot or cold, just the way Chickadee likes. Come on, I tell her, and I start to take off her little clothes. As soon I put her in the water, she starts to cry. It hurts, Maju. I guess it's her feet, I see them red underwater. She jumps up, moving her feet quick, as if the bathtub is still on fire. I know it hurts, it's going to pass, I tell her. She tries to get out of the bath, but I think about the day we've had, the amount of germs on this child, and I hold her arms. Soon I realize I must not force my Chickadee. She gets more nervous and starts to cry louder. To say: I want my mom. It's the first time she's said this since we left. It makes me sad and also worry, what if someone hears it. I say: it's O.K., Ana. I'm not Ana, I'm Cora and I want my mom, now she screams with the strength that can only come out of anger, and with that same strength she finally gets out of the bathtub. I get a towel to cover her, you can't walk around naked in the cold, but she doesn't want to hear of it, it's like a spirit possesses her, she runs to the bed and now I'm the one who screams: stop it, Cora, don't go lie on that filthy mattress with your foo foo naked like that. She doesn't care. I run between her and the bed, quickly pull the sheets before she can lie on them, while my bag flies out and hits the wall.

It was open, my bag. I hear it. Before I even turn around, I already know my Lady is gone. I know that sound of dry clay breaking, like plant pots at the farm. It can only be my Lady. I have a look, all my things all over the floor, my fake pearls roll everywhere, one under my feet. And next to it, a piece of my Lady's veil. I tell my Chickadee to leave the room, there are shards everyone, she'll cut her foot. She jumps on the bed, crying. I crouch down, praying the rest will be intact, my Lady, please make my Lady be safe, but as soon as I grab the bag I see more pieces underneath it, a head to one side, a veil to the other, the feet pushed in a corner. I hold my Lady's head in my fingers. Is this a sign? I start to think about everything that's happened. Cora has had Bibi since she was two years old and had never lost the sheep. I had never lost a saint in my life, I came from Mandaguaçu with an image of Saint Expeditus inside my bra, I still have the piece of paper in my wallet, but today I lost my Lady then broke the other saint. And still I didn't listen. My Lady had to make this whole scene, this tantrum from Cora, who looked more like she'd been possessed by some great force, just to call my attention. What are you trying to tell me? I ask, looking into the one eye that's still there. Are you with me? There's no answer. Not that I'm waiting for a miracle, for the Virgin to appear in a love motel or to talk through a tiny clay mouth, but maybe she can show up in my head, like she has so many times when I felt her whispering in my mind. But nothing, my mind is blank. My Lord, are you with me? I say and look up. I see a strange image. Not Jesus or my Lady, or the ceiling or the sky. I see myself, Our Lady broken, and Cora in the mirror. And as I see us, I realize Our Lady and Jesus Christ are talking to me, because missing the bus was a sign, losing the sheep and my Lady was a sign, seeing the satanic dog on the road was a sign, the broken saint was another sign, and the mirror is one too. A way to make me look up and open my eyes to what I'm doing, on my knees on this filthy carpet picking up the pieces of a saint, with a daughter who is not mine crying naked on a love motel bed.

Looking at this twisted image in the mirror, I feel my heart race. The more I think the more it speeds. It's a strange feeling, because I try to calm down, but my chest won't stop. Like it has a life of its own. I worry, I've never felt this before, is this a heart attack? Just thinking this my heart races again, my body is out of control. I can't think well anymore. I can't think at all, only feel, my hands sweating, my fingers dizzy, heat climbing up from my chest to my head and taking my breath away. I had a boss who died from a heart attack. Who's going to take care of this child? This thought makes it even worse. My heart beats so so so so fast it feels like my whole body is just heart. I start praying. I hold my Lady's head with all my strength, my eyes closed, don't let me go, my Lady, not now. And believing I was heard, that my faith can save me, I feel my heart slow down a bit. It's still racing, but it feels it's getting better, at least a little, the air coming back to me, at least a little.

I open my eyes slowly. Is it life? Thank God it's life, all twisted, but life. Cora is looking at me scared, my finger bleeds from squeezing my Lady's sharp head. Only now I realize I was on my knee this entire time. I let go of my body and fall to the ground. I cry out of relief. Cora comes next to me. She hugs me and says: don't cry. You can call me Ana if you want, I won't get mad.

I sit Chickadee down on my lap, after all I've been through, it's so nice to sniff a child's head, this child's head. The tears keep falling down my face, like they're coming to clean my windows, now I can even feel my Lady whispering in my mind, a clarity that I can't have alone. I realize the huge divine intervention that just happened. After sending me all those signs and making me see how this day looked like from above, divine providence sent me its great message. Because of course it's not normal for someone to have a heart episode that goes nowhere. How is it possible, to get close to death and then return safe? That was God intervening so I realized what will happen if I die. Especially after making the new documents. I don't have any family, I don't have energy to go find a step father for Cora,

I don't even have eggs to give her a brother. If I pass on, she'll end up in an orphanage or have to become a slut or somebody's maid. She'll be a woman in a little maid's room. A silkworm that can dry up in her tiny cocoon and no one even notices. Is that what you want for this child, for her to be like . . . I think and look up, at my hair frizzy from all the sweat. If Cora was still a baby I found on the streets like Neide's, but no, she has a family, and people who can give her everything I can never offer. Why didn't you think of that before, woman? Because it was all so fast, I answer out loud, and start to cry again. Cora wipes off my tears. Stop it, Maju. You're forty-four years old, you're already a teenager, she says, repeating a phrase she heard from her cousin. I think of her family, of the tree I'm chopping down with an axe, which only confirms what I must do.

I get up, tell her she doesn't have to take a bath anymore. I go to the sink and wet a towel from Big Corn. I wipe Cora's body with the towel. I put on her clothes, and to give her a fresh feel, I brush her hair. Then I turn down the lights, tuck her in bed, a pillow under her head, her sheep in her arms. She asks me to pet her air, something she asks me every night. She must be tired, because as soon as I touch her head, she falls asleep.

Better this way, I think. I don't want her to see me desperate like this. What happened was bad, but there's more to come. I already understood what I must do, but how? I ask for another light and nothing happens. I just hear the TV on low. I realize the divine providence has already done its part, to save this girl, now it doesn't matter what happens to me. I walk around the room, look for a window. Whenever I had something on my mind, I liked to lean on the window in my little maid's room, but here there isn't a single opening on the wall, I've never seen something like it. I stop to look at my phone. It's ten thirty at night, the screen full of notifications for unread texts and missed calls. I decide not to read or listen to anything, what if the device will give out my location, show where I am?

I feel angry toward Mrs. Fernanda. All this is her fault. I may be in my room right now, reading Nora's book, Chickadee sound asleep with Bibi in her room. Right, I didn't have to eavesdrop on her conversation, but who can resist a half-open door? I was leaving Cora's room when I heard my name coming from the master suite. I went into the closet in the hallway and pretended I was arranging the linen, while I eavesdrop on a conversation between Mr. Cacá and Mrs. Fernanda. I knew she was mad at me. The day before Cora had a birthday party after school and I said I can't bring her, I had a conjugal visit. Lauro had already abandoned me, I wasn't going to make productive love with anyone, but I had scheduled a mani-pedi with this woman who came to people's houses and was traveling far, I can't stand her up. Or lose the thirty-five reais. Val didn't charge much, but if you canceled at the last minute, you must pay anyway. So I kept the appointment, if I don't sleep at home today, my husband will kill me. Mrs. Fernanda put her hand on her waist. I have to supervise a shoot, what am I going to do? I stayed quiet. The other maid, who can maybe help out, had already left and Mr. Cacá had to deliver some cactus at a wedding, I didn't have any suggestions. I remember she looked at her phone and sighed, her eyes tearing up. I thought it was weird, Mrs. Fernanda had always been so strong, I had never seen her upset like this because of work. But I didn't even want to know what the problem was, I grabbed my purse and left before she can tie me down to the Tokyo Suite.

The next day, the conversation in their bedroom. I guessed something was wrong, because my boss was so upset, the shoot must have been horrible, it looked like she was hit by a car while she slept, her eyes swollen, her robe all messy, a boob almost jumping out. She didn't even say good morning, she was mad at me. In the hallway, I heard her say she was going to fire me. Mr. Cacá told her to calm down, she was the one who came up with that conjugal visit business. Mrs. Fernanda said it was true, she had come up with it, but it hadn't worked, she needed someone she may count on day and night. Mr. Cacá suggested talking to me, maybe I will agree to that. I think Mrs. Fernanda was walking around the room in that moment, I just heard Mr. Cacá asking her to cool down before making any decisions.

Nothing was decided yet, but I started to panic. I left the sheets in the closet and went back to my cocoon. I thought about the money. It's the first thing we think about. It wasn't the first time I was fired, I'll make it work. The problem was Cora, never see my Chickadee again? I had already gone through that with another child, Mrs. Natália's Totô. She sent me away because she got divorced and was left high and dry, there wasn't even money to buy toilet paper, let alone pay for a nanny. I was crazy about Totô, Totô was crazy about me. We said I'll come back to see the little boy. The first time, the child jumped on my neck and Mrs. Natália welcomed me like I was a guest. Six months later I showed up with a gift, it had been Totô's third birthday. He didn't even recognize me. He got the helicopter I gave him and ran to his room, Natália uncomfortable with my presence, in a hurry to go do something else. I quickly drank my water and left; the little rascal didn't even want to say goodbye. So Mrs. Fernanda won't even have to bother with all that "my house will always be open to you" bullshit, because that won't work on me, maybe go find another idiot to try that on. And what's a visit when we can be with someone all the time? I loved Cora in a way it had never happened with another child. That day, I went to the tiny window in my little room and looked out. I thought that this forbidden love between baby and nanny was also Mrs. Fernanda's fault. She had left her child in the corner of her life, and in that corner was me.

22

I didn't dwell on it long before deciding. It was best not to go. I'd stay in the corner, a satellite around all those people from Mato Grosso do Sul who've known each other for years. Sucking up to the poet. Nice cover, nice verses, can I get an autograph? And all this discomfort for what, just to mark my territory, something that made no difference with Yara, and on top of that to add more images of Yara flirting with other people to my private mental album? Better I stayed home with two slices of cucumber on my nipples and get back once Violeta left.

Another advantage of staying home was dismissing Maju for the rest of the day. I was mad at her for having left the previous day, I couldn't even look at her. I said she could go, I'd take the afternoon and evening to do something with my husband and daughter. That being said, we went on with our program: a trip to the mall. I don't know what humanity has done to end up like this. After going through so many wars, surviving so many epidemics, inventing penicillin and airplanes, we reach our apex as a civilization by walking through narrow hallways and dodging elbows to see clothes on sale. It wasn't what I wanted to do, but it was Cora's idea, and on a Saturday afternoon, a child's vote is worth more than an adult's. On top of that, Cacá also wanted to go, he needed to buy God knows what. Or that was just an excuse to go to the nearest place, with AC and easy parking.

As soon as we arrived, we saw a dog. A pug wearing weird clothes—the fact that a dog was wearing clothes is already plenty weird to me, but this was even more so—a skirt with red and golden frills. Cora loves dogs. She crouched down to pet the doggy. The owner proudly said: she's dressed as a rumba dancer, then explained her pet was taking part in a costume contest in the mall's atrium. Cora squealed with joy. I looked at Cacá and through the telepathy we developed by spending so much time together, we agreed the contest would be a drag, but we couldn't deny our daughter this pleasure.

In the atrium, I found out it wasn't just her and half a dozen people who were interested in the contest. The seats around the stage were nearly all filled, it took us a while to find three open seats. Right in front of us was a friend of Cora's. The two of them sat together. Cacá, the girl's mother, and I sat in the row behind. How lucky she sat next to my husband, because not only was I not in the mood to chat, I wasn't in the mood to chat with her. She was a holistic mother, one of those who bakes her own bread, squeezes fruit for her own organic juices, and makes toys with reforested wood, unintentionally setting up such a high standard for motherhood that it sets us all back. In order to be this perfect, we'd all have to give up our professional life and go back to household obligations, voluntarily binding ourself to the stove. While she talked about how she was trying to make terrariums at home with her daughter, my phone buzzed. Are you coming to the book launch? We're getting ready, we leave in a bit.

I liked that Yara reached out but telling me that they were getting ready together set in motion my editing brain.

SCENE 1—YARA'S BEDROOM—DAY

Yara bare-chested, putting on pants. Violeta comes near her with a joint. She places it between Yara's lips. While she takes a puff, their bodies brush against one another, Yara's nipples get hard.

SCENE 2—YARA'S BEDROOM—DAY

Violeta puts on a dress. She asks Yara to zip her up. Yara moves close, looks at the opening on her back, which goes up her spine starting over her butt. Yara gets on her knees and pulls down the dress.

When I came to, the holistic mom was talking about natural fermentation. I too was fermenting, not only with jealousy but with lust. Imagining the two of them had made me wet, and I don't know why but being wet at ten to six in the afternoon at the mall felt like a crime. I was so uncomfortable with my body and my inability to have a conversation that I decided to go to the restroom and freshen up. But not having Cacá and the holistic mom grounding me to reality was worse. I went on thinking about Yara and Violeta while I entered the stall and tried to pee. Then it occurred to me that the button was between my legs, that pressing it might turn me off. The only time I had masturbated in a public place was in an airplane toilet on a flight to Tokyo when I didn't know what to do with my hands anymore.

I got up and leaned against the wall. I thought of Yara and touched myself. A line must have formed because at one point someone got annoyed I was taking so long and asked: everything O.K. in there? I remember thinking: fuck me, I can't even masturbate in peace in a mall bathroom. I said everything was fine and continued touching myself until I came to the sound of flushing and hands drying.

I left the bathroom like nothing had happened and went back to my seat. The contest had begun and the host was thanking the sponsors and explaining the criteria for the prize. I sat down, relieved after the orgasm and also taken by that feeling of incompleteness that follows. It's not that I think we're incomplete, we're whole even if precariously, but post-orgasm melancholy is a thing, I have no doubt, because it's what I was feeling after having merged and made love to Yara, even if only in my mind. Maybe that subtle sadness was also intensified by the growing realization, each day more obvious, that I'd never have that woman. That she'd eventually slip away with her travels, parallel relationships, and adventures she'd never give up. It was exactly her free nature that I loved so much, which paradoxically bound me to her. And who was I? In that moment, just a woman watching a dog contest.

The first contestant to walk the runway was a medium-sized mutt with a cowboy hat and a cartridge holder around its stomach, led by a teenager. The audience clapped, Cora even screamed, and I liked seeing her cheer. Then came a tiny candidate, perhaps a puppy, dressed as Super Man and draped in a red cape. The hero was startled by the audience, got stuck at the stage entrance, its owner pulling the leash in vain. She had to carry the dog in her arms and still, or maybe for this very reason, she got a round of applause. Next, a dog dressed as an astronaut, led by a boy also in an astronaut costume. They got a standing ovation because of their great costumes, both in overalls, helmets, and NASA patches. The following contestant was a dog wearing a hat and a clown nose, followed by the rumba dancer we'd met. And then a small and aloof mutt, wearing a black wig with a curly tuft of hair and a white blazer studded with colorful stones. I don't know exactly why but the dog in the Elvis costume made me cry. A cry triggered by the underlying sadness of that contest but also filled with so much more, as all crying tends to be, rip tides taking everything with them.

I couldn't contain myself. Or maybe I didn't want to. I let the tears run down my face. Cora was too distracted to notice but Cacá did and looked at me with simpathy. To my surprise, he said: it'll pass, and put his arm around my shoulders. In that moment, I had the feeling that he knew about Yara, that he had heard me say "I love you" on the phone, that he had read all the signs I'd given away. And even suspecting, he wisely chose not to corner me—what good would that do? I felt love for my husband, a love I hadn't felt in a long time. I nestled against him, regretting the mechanisms of marriage, the dynamics that both generate and erode love. Or was it only a matter of time, the inevitable erosion that comes with time? I had no idea, because even thought I made documentaries, went to therapy or thought about love, I'd never come close to dissecting it. To me, whatever generated or ruled love was inexplicable, like the orchestration that causes birds to fly in flocks creating shapes. All the elements that had once attracted me to Cacá were still there: his sense of humor, his dedication, his ability to talk about any topic; but the adjectives didn't harmonize with one another anymore, they no longer formed shapes. They meant nothing to me. And what a pity they didn't, because for me it would be easier to go on loving my daughter's father than to love somebody else. But it was Yara I wanted and it was her I was thinking of when I saw someone place a trophy on an astronaut's paw.

23

I ready to leave. I like to look nice, I never leave the house without checking I look presentable, but now more than ever I needed to look like I'm a decent woman, not a lunatic who's kidnapped somebody else's child. I stop in front of the bathroom mirror, wet my hands, pat down my hair. My hair can tell when I'm nervous, maybe it's the humidity from all the tears, these electric wires sprouting from my head. I pat it down, put it up in a bun. I don't have any makeup, but I wash my face with water, brush my eyebrows.

Then I take all my few belongings, the things I found on the way—the fake jewelry, the ketchup packets, the bottle opener, the pen, the little Forbidden Fruit bottles all over the floor. And the pieces of my Lady, what to do with them? Leaving it on the floor is wrong, I don't want to belittle Our Lady. I pick up the pieces to throw out, but that's even worse. If abandoning her is disrespectful, throwing her out is the baddest. I want to bury her, for you are dust and to dust you shall return, a cross made of toothpicks stuck in the earth, a goodbye prayer and some plants covering it all afterward. That's a beautiful ending, but I don't have time or earth for this. We never have the earth for anything, we're always so far from where our feet must not have left, maybe that's why we suffer so much. Tell me, my Lady, what do I do with you? If I leave her on the nightstand, someone can find her and glue her back. Poors are so good at bringing things back to life. But maybe they'll throw her away. Maybe is best to leave it all under the bed, I bet a motel maid doesn't bother cleaning under there, sweeping and vacuuming like you do in someone's home. My Lady will be forever under this bed, and then I start to imagine the number of things her saint ears will overhear, maybe that is hell, dying and staying stuck under a bed where no one ever sleeps.

Since I don't know where to put my Lady, I decide to bring her. She doesn't fit in my purse. I wrap her in the plastic bag where I found the towels, a tight knot on top. I look around the room to see I don't forget things. Then I throw my bag under my arm, pick up Cora, the plastic bag in hand. With so much stuff I can just open the door, no way I will close it, the maid can fix that later. I walk quickly, the child's weight gets worse with each minute, I know that in an hour I must stop.

When I get to the motel's entry, there's a car waiting to check in and I have to wait behind it. I look down because of all the cameras. The car leaves and I move forward. The reception guy looks like he's seen a ghost. You were staying here at the motel? I say I was in the Orchid suite and rest Cora on the counter so I can grab the money. I'm afraid I'll get caught if I use my card. He does the math, the food, the drinks, he gives me the total through a little drawer, still staring at me in shock. I give him the money and ask if he can call me a cab. He continues staring at me while he dials the number. Suddenly I'm scared he's calling the police. Hello, the fugitive is here with me, call for backup. I discreetly knock on the counter, the man notices it. And my knocking must do something, because no one picks up. And if no one picks up, the man is really calling the cab company. It's difficult at this hour. It seems any hour is difficult, I complain, annoyed. My plan was to go to a bus station. Depending on the price, maybe get a cab to my final destination. But sometimes we have a plan and God has another. In my case, God always has another. I ask where there's a bus stop and leave the motel on foot.

I walk a few blocks. Maybe this isn't much for someone who

has their hands free, but I'm carrying a child turned cement sack, I feel sweat drops down my forehead. I arrive at the bus stop feeling that I can't take another step. I sit Cora on the bench. Then I take off my coat, cover her small body. I notice that one of her shoes, the one that was folded down on the heel, has fallen off. That's just what we needed, how am I going to find a shoe in the dark? I look around, the sky is light because of the moon, maybe I will see it. I hold onto my Lady and walk to one side, then the other, I use the flashlight on my phone, I even find horse shit, but can't see her shoe anywhere. It must have fallen somewhere else, and I even think of going look for it, but I can't leave her alone or risk missing the bus. I go back to the bench, imagining the shoe fallen in a corner. It's what people lose the most, what they have on their feet. I know because my shy makes me walk with my eyes to the ground and I've seen everything that's been lost out there, hats, glasses, keys, hair clips, IDs, packs of pills. I've even seen knives and playing cards. But nothing tops the number of shoes. Everywhere there's one, an alone shoe. And I always thought about what kind of state someone had to be to lose a shoe, because you can leave behind anything in life, a husband, a house, a city, a whole past, but not the very thing that will take you on your journey. Someone who leaves a shoe behind has not hope anymore.

I'm not at that point yet, of leaving behind my shoes. God willing, soon a bus will come and take me somewhere where I can find a cab. It's just the cold is hard. I rub my arms. Then I make sure Cora is comfortable, I try to wrap my jacket around her like a sleeping bag, but I can't do it because something distracts me. It's Mr. Cacá calling again. The buzzing from my phone gets on my nerves. I stick it in my bag and go back to staring at the road.

24

Just before midnight, the phone rings. It's my sister, calling from the farm. For some reason, I have the feeling that something is wrong. Maybe it's how slowly she says my name. She tells me that Cora isn't there. And mom, has she heard from her? My sister says she hasn't. They are worried. They'll have a bite, a quick rest, and get on the road to São Paulo. I hang up and tell Cacá. He grabs his phone and wallet and says: let's go to the police. I don't even get changed. I leave in sweatpants and flip flops, only grab my purse. I press the elevator button several times. We get in. The ride from the third floor to the ground has never felt so long, the walk from the elevator to the car has never felt so long.

Cacá turns on the car, and speeds out the garage. I say: fuck, what could have happened? It can't be good, he says. We start going over theories. When he stops, I continue.

There was only one kid.
Someone drew a gun,
The kid died,
and then there were none.
There was only one kid.

Stop it, Fernanda, you idiot, I tell myself. I roll down the window, take a deep breath. Good thing the police station isn't far. Soon we park on Angélica Avenue. We walk quickly, go through the gates of the 14th precinct. With every step a new reality, sad and maybe irreversible, seems to cement itself. I consider not walking through the door, as if denying a fact could save it from existing, but I move on.

We rush to the front desk. Our daughter is missing. A cop turns around to look at us: how old? Four, Cacá answers, faster than me. The man frowns. Four is bad. A second ago there was a mother reporting a twenty-two-year-old missing. A twenty-two-year-old isn't usually anything bad. But anyway, we'll help you in a moment, he says, and points at a waiting room with a few chairs.

I can't sit down. How can someone sit in such a situation? Not even Cacá, our resident monk. He paces up and down the room, drinks a glass of water. My phone buzzes, I hope it's a text from Maju. Mrs. Fernanda, we came to sleep at so and so's house, sorry I didn't tell you before. But it's Yara saying good night and sending me a slap on the butt. I have the urge to tell her what's happening. I can't do it in front of Cacá, though suddenly everything seems so irrelevant: the crisis in my marriage, my husband, Yara herself. I step out for a moment and quickly talk to her. Then I get back to the waiting room.

The chief of police calls us in. First, he asks us to give our information to the clerk. Just like the elevator ride, my name feels endless, spelling the many consonants of my Polish last name has never bothered me this much. They also want to see Cora's ID. Cacá says we don't have it. It's the nanny who takes care of our daughter most of the time, and carries the ID with her, along with her health insurance card. At any rate, we give him Cora's information, full name and date of birth, physical appearance. But when it comes to Maju, we don't have everything. Not even I who hired her can remember her full name. I only know it's Maria Júlia, brown hair, brown eyes, white skin, average build, forty-four years old, the same age as me. The chief says it's fine, we can send him what's missing when we get home. The important thing now is for him to understand the case.

Cacá takes over. He explains a bit of Cora's routine with Maju, says that this Monday wasn't any different: the two of them left early, right after breakfast, to get a cab downstairs and go to the club where our daughter has swimming lessons. The chief asks if we saw them leave. We say we didn't, but that the other maid did and didn't notice anything unusual, except that the nanny was carrying a big bag and a Tupperware. This isn't strange because, besides Cora's clothes and a towel, Maju likes to bring cut fruit for a snack. They also took Bibi, I add, explaining that's what made us believe they might have gone on a trip with my mother. The chief asks if that's unusual, taking the sheep. We say not really, when Cora is moody, we let her leave with the sheep. He looks at Cacá for a moment, he's already understood who's who in our relationship, and asks him if Maju is trustworthy. Completely, Cacá answers, and I agree, adding that she's been with us for three years. The chief asks if we know which driver took them to the club. We say we don't, but that it would be easy to find out as it must be someone from the taxi rank. Then he asks if we called the club and the school to check if they'd been there. Cacá says we haven't since up until a moment ago we thought they were at the farm, and we ran to the police as soon as we realized they weren't. Then the chief wants to hear about our financial situation. I tell him where we live, that we have a Renault. He asks if we've received any strange phone calls, any call from a private number. I say we haven't. He looks at the clock on the wall. He says it probably isn't kidnapping. Besides our lack of ostentatious wealth, were it that kind of situation the kidnappers would have contacted us by now. Though of course you never know, especially in a country with such creative and varied extortion techniques. After this, he advises us on what to do in case we receive such call.

Then the chief looks down at some illegible scribbles on a piece of paper in front of him. He continues: and this Maju, do you know if she's in any kind of financial trouble? I say she isn't, as far I know. And it's unlikely, since we pay her very well. Maybe she could have some kind of debt, a son who is involved with drugs, he suggests, and I realize he's on the wrong trail, suspicious of someone who's beyond suspicion. Cacá probably feels the same because he immediately replies that Maju doesn't have kids. She is happily married, trying to get pregnant, and has no reason to get into trouble. The chief then asks us about our building staff. Cacá mentions Chico and Aldo, quickly adding we don't think they're involved.

The chief wants to know if we have any hunches. It might seem ridiculous, he says, but sometimes the solution for a case is inside people. Cacá gives a nervous laugh and says he'd love for the solution to be inside him. I say I also have no clue, but I'm afraid it might be a robbery of some kind. I finally put on the table my repressed anxiety, and ask: do you think it's possible they were killed? For the first time, he looks at me with pity. I understand that yes, it's possible, and I have the urge to rush to the restroom. I hold it in, I'm not leaving this room before I've heard everything. What else could it be? I ask. He answers: maybe they were accident victims and for whatever reason their documents weren't found. Victims, Cacá answers, staring into space, and I feel like he's about to cry. I put my hand on his thigh. The chief says it could also be a disappearance, vanishing without any explanation. I ask if that's common. He says more than you'd think. We don't hear much about it because the mothers of missing kids are often ashamed to share their stories. They're like the mothers of kids who've drowned, they think it's their fault even when it's not. Then he asks for some more details, gives us a copy of the police report and tells us to stay calm. They'll put everything in the system, check hospitals and police stations, in less than three hours they should have more information and will call us.

As soon as we leave the room, I run to the restroom. I don't even check if the seat is clean. I sit down and, much to my surprise, I take a shit. A big one. Then, still sitting on the toilet, I look at my phone. Maju's messages, which I tried so hard to ignore over the past few years, are now all I want. I text her: where r u? where r u? where r u? Even though I don't hold out much hope she'll respond.

When I get out of the bathroom, I find Cacá waiting for me. We walk in silence out to the street. By the car, there's a newsstand. I quit smoking years ago, but fuck all the effort I've made. I ask for a pack of Marlboro red, I want the strongest ones they have. I also buy a lighter. The man at the stand points at a box of Bics, asks me what color. I say it doesn't matter. I hand him the money and take a few steps on the sidewalk. Cacá has never smoked, he hates the smell of cigarettes, but he asks me for one. It's cold, windy, we need to make a little tent with our hands to light each other's cigarettes. I look at Cacá's tense face. This man has been my boyfriend, my husband, my friend, sometimes even my father. Now he's also my brother.

25

The bus is no show yet, so I look at my phone again. A new message on the screen: where r u? where r u? where r u? I don't know. Why I looked at this crap. I put it back in my bag. It's not only the messages that make me nervous, it's also all this wait. I'm used to São Paulo, buses coming and going no matter the time. It's like in Mandaguaçu over here, if there's a bus in your lifetime, another will only come after you're dead. And two are already gone. Is that really it, no more coming tonight? It's past midnight, I can't wait anymore.

I never thought of hitchhiking, it's for the reckless, but now I must consider it. What else can I do? Of course I won't go with just anyone, the number of murdered people I've seen on TV, my God. Must I stop a car or a truck? Maybe a car, a woman will be the bestest. But in this dark, how can I know if it's a woman inside the car? I can't tell even if there's a giraffe. All I can see is what type of car. It's best to signal a newer model. The car of a person who works, makes money, has air freshener hanging from the rearview mirror. Mess is the first sign of crazy: people are so out of it they forget to take care. So no way I'll go on this Variant that drives by, falling apart. The car that comes after is also suspicious, too long, it looks like a funeral car, what's this lunatic carrying in the back? Then the road is empty. I look at the clock, 12:06 A.M. 12:09. 12:13. Then lights appear and I recognize the model, a Chevy Prisma just like Lauro's, the car of someone who pays their bills on time. I raise my hand and stick out my thumb like they do in the movies. The Prisma stops. A twenty-something guy rolls down his window. He seems a good person, his hair neatly combed back. Where are you going, ma'am? I take a peek inside the car, everything looks normal, no guns, no knives, no chainsaw, but I'm still so so scared. Once I'm inside the car I won't have any control. Where are you going? he repeats. I'm not going anywhere, I was just waving. The man sighs and takes off.

I feel a wave of tired. Like maybe I must give it all up. Looking for a ride, life. It will be great, just turn everything off like it's a machine. Live a little and then come back to live more when it hurts less. If Cora wasn't here, I will stay here until I run out of battery, until I die of hungry or cold or until someone picks me up. Or until they don't pick me up, like trash in places God's forgot, where people and a plastic bag are all the same. And speaking of plastic bags, there comes another truck, the Elma Chips face smiling at the road. I think: why not? Maybe it's even better. The driver is an employee, with cargo to deliver, a schedule to follow, he won't be raping during his shift. To show that I'm an honest woman, I go over to the bench, grab Chickadee. I come back with her sleeping in my arms, I raise my hand. Another comes and drives right by me. Soon after comes a car carrier. This one will stop, it's carrying so many cars, what difference will it make to add a woman and a girl? It must make some difference, because the driver doesn't stop. Maybe he didn't see us. I decide to walk a bit further, my right foot on the yellow line on the pavement.

Here comes another one and I think it was sent for me, on the bumper there's a sticker saying "God is watching over me." But this one doesn't stop too, or the tractor-trailer or the tanker that come after. What on earth is happening, life has made these people so evil. After a few minutes, another one comes. To my surprise, the truck brakes. The door opens. A man looks down at me. I'm scared of him, but he looks scared of me too. He watches me, suspicious, from his seat covered in wooden beads—like the ones Lauro had in his taxi to help him relax in traffic. I'm going to São Paulo, I tell him. Me too, hop on, he says, and offers his hand to help me up. I don't know if it's his kind or the seat like Lauro's, but I'm not too scared of him, only a little. I sit down, settle in the seat without waking up Chickadee, put on the seat belt. Is that your daughter? he asks. I say yes. He takes off, the motor roaring.

Then he asks me what a woman like me is doing on the road, at this hour. I say I was mugged at the convenience store. I left my suitcase for a second while I gave the girl her dinner and someone took it. I say that all my money was in there, our documents. That's why I decided to go back to São Paulo. He says the road is full of criminals, he knows it well. And people with no soul, I add, and then tell him I asked for a ride for half an hour and not a single trucker stopped. It's because you're with the girl, he says. If you were a skank they'd have stopped. I don't understand, I ask him what's a skank. He says it's a whore. They know it from the way you're dressed, by the way you get on the truck. Everyone comes into the cabin facing the driver, skanks come in sideways. I shake my head. He continues, and explains that none of the truckers stopped because a woman with a child asking for a ride has to be trouble. I ask what kind of trouble. Child abduction, he says. I feel my insides go cold, is it possible he knows? He said "abduction," the way a cop must call it. I imagined mutilation, rape, robbery, but never getting caught by a cop undercover as a trucker. I feign ignorance, child abduction? Yes, a lot more kids get abducted than we realize, he says, and looks at me. I'm so nervous I almost confess, you can handcuff me right here, sir. He continues: but from the way you're dressed, I can tell you aren't that kind of person. I let out a sigh of relief. He grabs a sleeve of pills. He pops one into his mouth, swallows it with water. Then he offers me the bottle. I'm so thirsty, but I'm embarrassed to tell him, I don't want him to think I take advantage, getting water for free, getting a ride for free. I thank him and say I'm O.K. Then I continue looking around the truck. He must live on the road, because the cabin is neat like it's his house. There's a Flamengo soccer club flag up on the ceiling. A picture of a woman on the dashboard. A blanket folded on the back seat. I watch him with the corner of my eye. He must be thirty something and not bad looking. Tan with a big face, if Neide was here she'll go crazy. He seems good. He asks me if I want to turn on the AC, if the temperature is good for the girl. But there's something weird about him. How he always moves, his fingers tapping on the wheel, always looking at the rearview mirror. Is he running away? I check the rearview mirror on my side—truck rearview mirrors are so big—but I don't see any cars behind us.

He asks me what I do for a living. I say I'm a maid, which is half true. I'm shy, but I keep the conversation going, the man lives alone on the road, he must be dying to talk to someone. And you, have you been doing this long? Since I learned to drive, he says. Then he tells he hasn't always drove this kind of truck, though. He started with a moving truck, then spent years with a grain truck, he carried soy, corn, that kind of something, a boring job because dry cargo is heavy, the driver needs to go very slow and he doesn't have the patience. I can tell, I almost say, looking at his index finger already tapping again, something he must always do, because the wheel is worn just where his fingers go.

26

We get into the car. I roll down the window, light another cigarette. In the meantime, Cacá calls the mother of one of Cora's classmates, Bebel. He explains the situation, I hear the despair in her voice on speaker. Cacá tries to soothe her, lying and saying that maybe Cora is sleeping at another friend's house. At any rate he asks her to wake up her daughter and ask if she saw Cora at school that morning. About five minutes later the mother returns and says the girl didn't see her. We know this doesn't mean anything; sometimes four-year-olds see a dragon battle but can't see the classmate sitting next to them. Following the chief of police's advice, we message the school group chat, explaining the situation and asking if anyone or their children have seen Cora.

I'm used to the quick pace of my own group chats, to the workaholics, to the gringos in other time zones, so I expect immediate responses, but it's almost two in the morning and apparently the parents of young children sometimes sleep. Cacá suggests retracing Cora and Maju's steps while we wait for any updates. From home to the club, from the club to school. Though I don't find it promising, I accept.

Cacá rolls down his window. We don't say a word. Our eyes peeled, our ears peeled. Driving slowly. He scans the left side of the street and I cover the other. It's one of those typical city blocks, with rows of townhouses. At this hour, there's no one on the streets. Only bright signs competing for attention in the limited urban space. We drive by Vivian Eyewear, its roller shutters down. The mechanic's rolling doors are also down. On one side, there's a door that leads to the second floor, a Muay Thai gym with dark windows, which might not show anything even during the day. A little ahead, a gate with metal arrows conceals a narrow alley. A podiatrist's office has the rolling shutters only half drawn and it looks claustrophobic, like only legs and feet could fit there. The locksmith's place doesn't even have a façade, just a door and a yellow key in a blue cap explaining its purpose. Next to it, a candy store, a stationery shop. Around the corner, Taste Delivery, its metal rolling doors not entirely down, a beam of light coming from the gap the size of my palm, a motorcycle parked out front. And all this on a single block. If each door and each window in this city conceals a mystery, as banal as it may be, how many secrets are there in a city the size of São Paulo? The same city that had once fascinated me with its infinite possibilities now horrifies me.

SCENE 1—TASTE DELIVERY—EVENING

Maju goes in with Cora and asks if they sell pizza by the slice, the child could smell it from outside and wanted some. The man at the cash register looks at Maju, then at a delivery man sitting on a bench. The two of them exchange a smile. The man looks back at Maju.

CASH REGISTER GUY

The kitchen is closed, but we can whip up something.

The cash register guy goes into the kitchen, while the delivery man gets up and rolls down the metal door. The cash register guy comes back with a kitchen knife. He corners Maju against a wall, holds the blade against her neck.

CASH REGISTER GUY
Take off your clothes or we'll cut you and the girl.

Maju takes off her clothes. The delivery man comes closer, zips down his overalls. He pulls out his hard dick. Maju addresses the men.

MAJU
Not in front of her.

The cash register guy grabs the child, sits her down on his lap, covers her eyes with one hand. The delivery man presses Maju against the counter and sticks his dick in her ass. The cash register guy watches while he touches Cora with his other hand. The girl cries.

The light turns green and we leave Taste Delivery behind. I don't tell Cacá what I've imagined. It's not time to lose it, I need to pay attention to the street. I regret not having brought a Klonopin. As soon as the thought crosses my mind a drugstore appears. I'm not surprised though, there's a Drugs This or Drugs That at every corner, but in any case, I don't have my benzodiazepines prescription on me. I look inside at the obscene white light shining on colorful packagings, looking for a woman and a child, a woman and a child, but the counter is empty. Painfully empty. The façades keep coming—a closed bakery, a house with metal bars on the windows, followed by a garage with a metal gate entwined with a heavy lock.

SCENE 2—HOUSE—EVENING

The taxi driver stops at the sidewalk, opens the metal gate. He drives in, locks it again. Then he opens up the trunk. He takes an unconscious Cora in his arms and takes her inside. He crosses a living room with her, past the couch, coffee table, TV. In the back, there's another door he unlocks with his free hand, revealing steep stairs. He goes downstairs careful not to trip, not to drop the girl. Downstairs there's another door, thick, with two more locks he opens using the same set of keys. The door opens to reveal a tiny apartment with low ceilings. An eleven-year-old girl, with the very pale skin of someone who hasn't seen sunlight in years, is doing the dishes. She turns around as soon as she hears the door open. She comes close to see the child the taxi driver brought with him, a curious gaze but also vacant. The girl tucks a lock of Cora's hair behind her ear. Her thin and pale wrist is marked by dozens of fine scars.

I remember the women who killed the monkey. I feel this force I've never felt before, not even when I gave birth. I feel like I can do anything. Tear a house off the ground, a building off the pavement like Godzilla, look into every nook and cranny of every building until I find Cora. I only stop myself because I'm not large enough, my hand is too small to prop open a roof or pop off the top of a building. I feel like if it came to it, I could even fly, though I can't fly out of my own madness. "Madness" isn't the right word. Everything I imagine while we go through this maze of doors and windows is possible, it's happened to other girls before. I get another Marlboro, light it, and take a drag with such force the ember eats up a third of the cigarette at once. I shouldn't be looking at the buildings. Cora and Maju probably aren't there anyway and even if they were, I wouldn't be able to see them. I should be looking at the sidewalks, at the places where I might find them. And that's what I do, block after block, ignoring the lit windows trying to lure me, until I see an overpass. And under it, three adults and about ten children wandering among mattresses, a grocery cart full of cardboard, and a bonfire.

SCENE 3—STREET—EVENING

Maju and Cora walk down the street during rush hour, the sidewalks thick with people. Maju stops and buys a bottle of water, gets distracted talking to the water guy. A woman takes Cora, who is quickly put in a grocery cart with the other kids, among all that trash. The cart moves through several streets until it arrives at an overpass. The woman dresses Cora in old clothes. Then tells her to go with a boy to ask for money at the traffic light.

SCENE 4—STREET—EVENING

Maju pays the water guy, turns around and realizes Cora is gone. In panic, she walks up and down the street. She goes into the stores, the subway station, the art gallery. She talks to a cop who asks for her ID. Maju gets scared, she walks away. Then she gets into a cab, goes to the station, and gets on a bus to Mandaguari.

I can still see the overpass in the rearview mirror. I throw out the cigarette and say: stop. Cacá doesn't understand. Stop the car right now, I know what happened. He obeys. I get out, slam the door. I walk quickly toward the overpass. From up close, the picture is even sadder. I suddenly understand for the first time the meaning of the word "poverty"—the ground covered in trampled packaging, young boys sucking on empty candy wraps. I'm not looking for them. I'm looking for her. I saw her back, her gait, her height, her hair. I start screaming: Cora, Cora. Everyone stares at me with their grimy faces. I walk over the torn mattresses, as if this place didn't belong to anyone, as if those people weren't anyone, only obstacles I had to dodge to find my daughter. Cora, mommy is here, I scream, as I step over a blanket. I arrive at a tent and realize I wouldn't need to tear it off the ground like Godzilla because it's already loose, no door and barely a roof to prop open. Cora, I repeat, touching the shoulder of the girl who I now see is not the girl I'm looking for. The girl looks at me confused. I hear Cacá calling me. I see our car parked in the middle of the street, the hazard warning on, my husband running in my direction. Let's go home, Fer. I feel his hand on my shoulder. His voice repeating: come on, let's go home. I think he apologises to the people who live there, I'm not sure. We walk together, we get in the car. I turn to him and ask: do you think we're going to find Cora? I do. You do? I do, he repeats. I really hope so, because having a missing child might be even worse than a dead one.

27

We haven't even been silent for a minute and he asks my name. Maju, I say. Then I think maybe I must lie. And yours? Ednardo. I know that name out of Lauro's mouth. Ednardo like the singer? Exactly, he says, and smiles with prideful, like he's the singer. Then he points at a picture on the dashboard. He says his mom was a fan. I stretch my neck to see the picture. He takes it from the dashboard, puts it on my hand. I tell him his mom is beautiful. He smiles with prideful again, everyone says that. Then he puts the picture back. He tells me her name was Samara. She died when he was fourteen. I tell him my mother died when I was five. He looks at me sad. He doesn't say anything, but I know what he's thinking—he feels lucky, nine more years to know her. But he also must pay the price for love—love is always so pricy—I see in his face that he misses his mother more than me. So much he keeps talking about her. He tells me she loved the song "Pavão Mysteriozo," do you know that one? I say yes and it's true, I remember Lauro in the living room with a dish towel on his shoulder singing the chorus. He says that was her favorite song, she listened to it every time she was hanging their clothes to dry, bringing the stereo in the backyard with an extension cord. I look at him and his mouth is dry and his eyes tearful. He takes a swig of water. When his mother was dying, he promised her he'll listen to the song every day for the rest of his life in her honor. And so he did for many years, listening to it every single day, no matter where or with who.

Until one Saturday he was arrested. I jump. Now I was calmer, he starts with that. Thank God, he quickly adds he didn't do nothing wrong. He smuggled appliances across the border without knowing, from Palotina to Guarapava, nine TVs with no receipts hidden in the middle of the other appliances. I check his face to see if it's true. Or maybe I want him to be true. In the end it's all the same. He continues explaining they tricked him, so he only spent one night in jail, just enough time for the police to catch the gang. That night I have this problem, how can I listen to "Pavão Mysteriozo?" The police station was small, that part was just a hallway with three cells. I was in the first cell with a weird man, who was squatting all the time. After they put him in there, Ednardo called the guard, said can you do me a favor. He was embarrassed to ask out loud, so he asked the guard to come close. The guard says no way, the last guard who befriended a jailbird was almost strangled through the bars. If you want to talk, you can talk from there. Ednardo cleared his voice and explained what he promised his mother, can the guard find a stereo or a cell phone, some way to play him the song? The guard was quiet for a few seconds. Then he burst out laughing and said: man, you're such a faggot! Ednardo heard laughs, whistles, voices screaming from across the three cells: faggot. He hadn't imagined so many people in the next cells, since he was put in the first, he hadn't seen the others. He shut up and stayed quiet like the man still squatting. It was late night and he didn't have much hope they'll let him out that day, so he asked sorry to his mother, telling her he's done many wrong things and she knew it, but he didn't know of any TV, or that he'll end the night there, with no toothbrush or "Pavão." After that, he tried to sleep, but the springs in the mattress groaned more than a dying man. Also, Ednardo always spent the night driving, so he can't go to bed this early. But good thing he can't, because a little later, when the station was quiet, when it must be almost midnight, he hears a voice. It came from the next cell. High-pitched, smooth, singing the first verse. "*Pavão misterioso, pássaro formoso . . .* " and so it continued, verse by verse, pause by pause, smooth until the end, "*eles são mutes, mas não podem voar.*" Ednardo thought they'll boo him, but no one, no one said a thing, not even the guard. The next day they let him go, without ever seeing the face of the man who sang for him. I see Ednardo's eyes are tearful again. This story also gave me chills. Or chilled my spine, like my nana liked to say. She didn't even like music, but she pops into my mind, called by the mysterious peacock in the song. I wonder for a moment if this story is really true, but why make that up? I don't know what to say, I just tell him I know the song. It's very beautiful. That it is, he says. Then he looks at the rearview mirror and continues, saying that he doesn't know if it's just with the lyrics to this one or that happens with any song, because he doesn't know any other so well, but it's interesting how each day or each period he sings it, the song has a new meaning. Like the road, which is never the same, it doesn't matter how many times you drive it. That night I spent in jail, the song was about a jailbird. "My beautiful bird, in the darkness of this night, help me sing. Get rid of this fire, get rid of this thunder, don't do anything that isn't right," he sings. And I think that he's wrong, the peacock is talking about Cora, about all the wrong things that I need to right. I don't know if it's from all the talking or the singing or what, but Ednardo's mouth is dry again. I can tell because his lips get stuck to his gums. He grabs the water bottle. Then he offers me some. I'm so thirsty, but I stay still, I can't with other people's germs, I wish I wasn't like this.

A gas station appears. Ednardo asks if I'm hungry. I say I'm not, I'll never make him stop the truck just for me. But I'm really not that hungry. I never am when I'm nervous like this. He says he skipped lunch, but he's also not hungry, but he needs to eat something to keep going. He slows down, drives into the station. He parks. He asks if I'll get out. I want to, but I can't. I'll have to bring Chickadee with me and I can't run the risk of waking her up. And no way I will leave Cora alone in the car. I'm so afraid of running out of oxygen with the windows closed like this. I'm so afraid of getting robbed when the windows are open. I'm so afraid of Ednardo leaving me and taking her. Staying in the cabin is my only choice. I ask him to buy me a water and a pastry. I discreetly put my hand in my bra, put twenty reais on his hand. He says he'll be right back and slams that heavy door.

I realize I have an opportunity here. An opportunity to see if he's an honest man. If I can go to São Paulo in peace. I wait for him to get into the store. I open the glove compartment, my hand shaking because I'm not the person to do this, in nearly thirty years working in people's homes I never snooped a drawer. But today it's different. I look inside, I find more pills, a pack of condoms, a CD with blue peacock feathers. And his employment record. I open the booklet and see his picture. He looks younger, even more handsome. I turn the page and get chills, already thinking his name is José Carlos, I'll have to run out with Cora. But his name is really Ednardo. Ednardo Pereira de Souza. The son of Maria Samara Alves Pereira and Rogério de Souza. I flip through, I do what I learned from my bosses, checking how long someone can hold a job, but before I can check the dates, I see him coming back. I quickly close the glove compartment, as he's getting each time closer, with two big bottles of water, a paper bag in his other hand. He opens the door. He hands me the bottle of Minalba and two pastries, says the other one is for the girl. I tell him that children this age take forever to wake up once they sleep. But thank you, when she wakes it's good to have something to eat. He also bought one for him. He eats it in two bites. He wipes his mouth with his hand. Is that all he eats? I think it's strange for a man so large to eat so little. I remember Lauro, he was like a bulldozer, but of course I don't say anything. Especially with my mouth full, chewing. When I'm done, I'm so thirsty I drink almost a quart of water. Ednardo takes another pill and drinks his Minalba.

28

We get home. Cacá tells me to go take a pill, but there's no need. It's the first thing I do, after quickly rummaging through my drawer. What a relief when I hear the blister pack pop, then feel the pill melt under my tongue. I think of taking two, but change my mind; I'd be too spaced-out and right now I can't, I have to be alert. I go back to the living room and find my husband on the phone. I assume it's a mother from the group chat who's seen the texts and wants to know what's happening. I can't hear her, but I feel her morbid curiosity in Cacá's detailed answers. My phone also has questions. From my sister, form Yara. I type short responses, I'm in a hurry, I want to give the police the information they requested. I open my laptop, look for copies of Maju's documents. I find her name, her social security card, her ID, her date and place of birth. Mandaguaçu, not Mandaguari. Then I look for her address, the chief said it was good to have it, but I can't find it. I also look for her on social media. Her only profile doesn't have any personal information or recent posts.

I go to her room, maybe I'll find something there. I open the door and turn on the light. It's so rare for me to go into the Tokyo Suite, the last time must have been when we renovated it. It was a well-thought-out design. To save space in the bathroom, we brought the sink to the bedroom, like they do in France. The sink is the first thing I look at, where I see a tiny sliver of soap. A very Maju thing to do, to use up everything until the very last bit. Her toothbrush isn't here, but I think it's normal, they have lunch at the club, Maju must have taken it. She's obsessed with hygiene. I turn around to look at her wardrobe, for a second I imagine it might be empty, that she took everything with her. It's a strange thought, I don't think she ran away with my daughter, she's trying to conceive, why would she and her husband take a child that isn't theirs? And if she were crazy enough to do something like this, she'd already done it. But now all kinds of crazy things cross my mind and when I open the door I'm scared. And indeed I have a reason to be scared, not because it's empty but because it's too full. My body recoils when I see the big, dark shadow I quickly realize is our Christmas tree. An artificial pine tree, even if disassembled, could never fit into my closet. It wouldn't fit anywhere, so it ended up here. Even though it isn't that big—Cacá had gone with the *slim* design—it fills up an entire section of the wardrobe. In the corner, there's only enough room for three hangers, with three t-shirts on them. Still, there are the drawers underneath. The first one is full of pants. In the second one, cotton panties with loose elastic bands, a pajama set that used to be mine, so faded now it looks almost white. I think it's interesting how she's so worried about looking nice and clean, and she makes good money, but has such worn clothes in here. Maybe it's poverty, that mark that never fully leaves, no matter how much money tries to erase it. I open the third and last drawer, hoping I'll find documents, maybe a bill with Maju's address. I'm surprised to find a collection of free stuff from places we've been to. Napkins from Starbucks, matchboxes from Riviera, chopsticks from Sushi Cute. Why on earth would a woman in Brazil need that many chopsticks? I don't know and don't want to know. I close the drawer and the wardrobe. I look around, there's no other furniture in the suite besides the bed. I kneel down but all I find under it is a pair of flip flops with thin soles from overuse. Then I remember how my great-grandmother used to keep money under the mattress. I lift the Ortosono mattress. On the slats I find a sea of books, placed side by side, so they don't budge. I grab one. *Dirty Deeds,* Hot Desire Series. For a moment, I forget the situation I'm in and smile. But only for a second, a fraction of a second. Then I put the book back, I look through a few others to see if I can find some non-fictional paper. There's nothing there so I go to the bathroom. I find another small chunk of soap, this one with a strand of hair on it, and a nearly-empty bottle of shampoo.

I leave the Tokyo Suite, walk through the living room. Cacá stops me, asks if I've found anything. I tell him I haven't, but I'll keep looking in the other rooms. I go into the bathroom. I see the footstool Cora uses to reach the sink. The cup where she keeps her toothbrush. It's empty, but again, that doesn't mean anything. Then I go to Cora's room, turn on the light. Inside is my girl's simple world. The wallpaper with colorful pennants, the light pendant shaped like a cloud. The small table Cacá painted because we couldn't find one that matched the color of the pennants. I walk past her small chair, stand in front of her closet. Cacá comes in. Let's see if they took her swim gear. He gets in front of me, opens the door. He knows exactly where to look. There are so many bikinis and swimsuits we can't tell if one's missing. Same thing with the goggles. Sometimes we forget to bring a pair on a trip and we just buy another one, she must have three or four, who can keep track. But she only has one swim cap with the club's logo. And it's there. Could they have forgotten it? Or could they have known they weren't going swimming? I remember her school bag, let's check if they took it. We start looking through the closet for her Kipling bag with the monkey keychain. We can't find it. The cap is there but the bag is missing, which sends us mixed signals. Still, Cacá informs the police.

In the meantime, I continue walking around the bedroom, I can't stay still. I decide to open the large drawers that store toys. I remember having organized those drawers, labeling them: dolls, instruments, animals, games, cars, play dough, others. A plan doomed to fail. Children collect so many trinkets, and nannies don't have time to differentiate between a jigsaw puzzle and a tangram—mothers even less. Nothing is further from real life than planning it. I open the big drawer labeled "others." I find dozens of small objects, items that don't fit into the other categories or that my daughter won't let us get rid of, like plastic lids, faux fruits, medals, a doll's arm, feathers from an old shuttlecock, crayon stumps, her baby shoes, cards, balloons, dry lumps of clay, layers of tiny things buried under one another with the remains of a Lilliputian hurricane. I dig my hands in, a bulldozer bringing more objects to the surface. I look at everything like I'm a confused and bereft detective. I stare at a whistle, a puppet made of paper drawings and chopsticks. I turn the chopstick in my hand. I remove its paper face, then fold it and put it in my pocket, if not like a clue, at least like an amulet. Then I go on opening every drawer, looking through toys, tossing rattlers, tambourines, and little pianos around. Cacá asks what I'm doing. I tell him I don't know. I feel small like my daughter. I decide to call my mother.

I've never gotten along with her, but suddenly I miss her voice. That rasp of someone who's smoked and drunk more than they should. Her inconsequential suggestions often more like counter-advice. Still, I call her. She answers on the speaker phone. She says she was about to call me. She's with my sister, they're on the way, anxious to know what's happening. I tell them about our visit to the police station. I explain we're waiting to hear from other stations, hospitals. My mom starts talking about something that happened with my father—how he once disappeared for almost twenty-four hours, and was found among the indigent at a public hospital with alcohol poisoning after a night of gambling. She gives us more details. My sister scolds her—your granddaughter is missing, this is not the time to be telling anecdotes. The two of them argue. I listen.

Their voices are like white noise, I've been listening to them argue for forty-four years. Typical mother-daughter stuff, complaining about one another, getting frustrated with one another, sometimes jealous of one another. And despite everything, together. Romantic relationships go, the honeymoon phase with sons cools down, but mothers and daughters cling to each other, prickling one another until their last breath. It's the most challenging relationship, but the most beautiful. I bite my lips, it's not the kind of thought I'd like to have right now. They call me: Nanda, are you there? I say yes, while I crouch down and hug my own knees.

29

I don't know what's gotten into this man. He's talking faster, opening his nose like an angry animal. I look at the road and don't see anything, his hunter must be inside his head. Or maybe he's in a hurry, because he also drives faster. And right when I need the bathroom. We drive by a gas station, but I don't have it in me to ask him to stop, I don't want to bother him. I must hold it for a bit longer. His rush isn't all bad, the soon we get there the better, but a part of me wants him to drive as slow as possible. To drive in circles, to take U-turns up and down the road for days on end, the sun going up and down, up and down, so I can smell this child's head for a bit more.

When I get my nose off Cora's hair, I see Ednardo is going even faster, the speedometer pointing down. To me that's already a safety issue. I work up the nerve and say, trying to sound casual: no need to hurry for us, O.K.? He looks at me. This thing's on its last legs. Legs? I don't know what he's talking about, maybe he's running from whatever is on his rearview mirror. Then he says it's best to get there early, because São Paulo is trouble. The trucks are only allowed to circulate for a few hours. Then he asks where we live. I tell him and he says he can take us there. I thank God for putting this man in my path. And if he is this kind, there's no reason for me to be embarrassed. I ask him to stop at the next gas station, I need to go to the restroom. He says that's fine and goes on talking, this time about his wife, his gem.

Maybe because you have to be a precious human to have a husband on the road, only coming home one or maybe two times a month. But his gem has cracked. She found another. I look at him and see his eyes tearful again—this one has even more emotions than me. He says she warned him, she tried to warn him. She was tired of being alone. Leave this trucker life or I'll find someone else. I think about my own situation, about how choosing work cost me my marriage. I ask if he considered quitting his job to stay with her. He said he didn't, because he'll go crazy without it. We can't control anything in life. On the road, at least, he has the illusion of control, that he's the one holding the clutch. I don't know what the clutch is, but I can imagine. He goes on and says that having to go somewhere gives meaning to the meaningless that's in everything else. If he spent his life on the same couch by the same window every day, he'll have to put a bullet through his head. I think: people are so different. For me, if they told me that every day of my life will be unexpected, that's when I'll put a bullet through my head.

I see a gas station, but it's on the other side of the road. I ask Ednardo if they got divorced, more to distract me from my bladder that's about to burst than out of curiosity. He says they're still together. You can learn anything in life, even to be a cuckold. He only asked her one thing, not to tell him, she can lie to his face if necessary, but to tell her lover that he knows. I might be a cuckold, but I'm not an idiot, he says, and his nose opens again. He keeps talking, but I can't pay attention anymore, my bladder is like a balloon full of water, the rubber wobbling with the weight, pressing its insides. I hold it with so much force my arm hair stands up. Each second becomes a minute. Time passes so slowly. And my body shows who is in charge. Anyone who felt real hunger or cold knows the power of the body. Everyone else finds out when they're real sick. Or in old age. But at one point everyone kneels down before their own carcass. I'm here on my knees in front of mine. When can we stop? I feel it drip, my pee wetting my underwear.

Can you stop the truck? I need to pee right now, I say. Ednardo shakes his head. He signals his turn and drives to the side of the road. I'm trusting Ednardo here, but I don't trust anyone with my eyes closed, not even the taxi drivers from our neighborhood. Even with them, I get in first and then Cora, because if there's something I learned watching the news is that lunies don't send you a memo before. I'll have to get out with her. Ednardo says: you can leave the girl, I'll watch her. I say: no, thanks, and get off the truck, looking for a place to pee on the edge of this corn field. Everything is so awful on this awful night, even the crops are dry, I hear the leaves crunching under my feet. At least there's a moon, showing me to a bush. I think of putting Chickadee down on the ground, but then remember there were snakes around the mulberry bushes back at the farm. I must pee with her in my arms.

Good thing I'm wearing a skirt, with pants it's impossible. With my free hand, I pull up the skirt, roll it up to my waist. Then I pull down my undies to the ground. I slip one foot out, then the other, then kick them to one side. I try to squat, but I can't, I fall, Cora is too heavy. The only option is to pee standing up. I open my legs wide. I can't believe I'm peeing like a man, my hips tilted forward so my feet won't get wet.

But I'm not a man, I can't even pee in peace, some pee splashes on my knees, my ankles, my shoes. Can Ednardo see us? I shake it off, I shake it off like a man. Then I try to get my panties from the ground but I can't reach it and I nearly fall. I also realize the underwear must be dirty anyway, covered in red dirt. I give it up. I drop my skirt. I go back to the truck and the smell of peepee follows me. Ednardo gives me his hand so we can get up there and his nose opens. Can he smell the stink? I'm always so careful about clean, I can't believe this is happening. I feel a wave of sad. Lonely. And Ednardo must be tired too, because he stopped chatting. He moves forward with his eyes all open, his fingers tapping on the wheel, but his mouth shut, clenched with that tension I can't figure out. I look at the clock on the dashboard. It's four in the morning. Won't you fall asleep at the wheel? I ask. Not at all, he says. I relax a little. My God, I'm so tired.

30

Mom, do you want to watch me swim? Do want to see me run from here to that wall? Cut this papaya with a knife? Put this whole French fry in my mouth? Dive in the bathtub? Roll my tongue? Wink? Do you want to see my pirate costume? Can you believe I can climb two steps at a time, mom? That I can reach the elevator button? That I can wipe myself? That I can write my name? That I can count to a thousand? That I can do a somersault? That I can put my plate on the sink without dropping it? That I can burp a, e, i, o, u?

Look at me dancing. Look at me jumping on the couch.

Look, look, look.

Look at me, mom.

31

I walk in the supermarket. I stop to a mountain of potatoes, I look at a few. I grab one, too soft. I grab another, no need to squeeze this one to know it's too old, look at the color, green. Number three is even worse, green and sprouting, little white crowns growing. I give up. I turn to the mountain of tomatoes. I grab one, red, shiny, but soon feel its skin is wrinkled. The lettuce, I don't even bother touching it, they're limp and dark. The papaya is rotten, full of dark dots. I go to the other side of the fruit stand, where everything seems fresh. The oranges catch my eye. I grab one. On the bottom, a green spot becomes white. No saving the strawberries either. The mold on them is a delicate frost covering the yellow seeds. I give up on all fruits and vegetables and go to the freezer aisle. I grab a bottle of milk. I look for the expiration date, but I can't find it. I open the cap and sniff it. Sour, curdled. I get a bag of sliced bread, peek through the plastic, mold. The flowers are dying too, but even in death they look prettier, no marks on their skin, only brown and fallen petals, too bad they crumble when I touch them. I decide to grab some pasta, nonperishables won't go bad. I grab the box and the penne falls out, the box has been eaten by bookworms, the penne by weevils, the bugs crawling through the pasta tubes, some of it already turned to powder. I put the box back on the shelf and realize the wood is rotting too, eaten by termites who run with the weevils. I start to despair, Cora must eat. I decide to look at the fish section, maybe there's something there. I push my shopping cart to the metal counter, where I see three whole sea basses. Lauro taught me to check the consistency if the fish is fresh, see the meat is firm. I touch one of the sea basses and my finger sinks in as if in a bowl of jello. I notice its gills look yellow, did it wink at me? I quickly walk away, past the meat section. The steak is on sale, so I grab a tray. The meat is almost blue. I never bought filet mignon, but today it's the only option. I grab a few. They don't look rotten, but I see the tiny head of a maggot in the middle of the marbling. Disgusting! I drop it on the ground. Only then I realize my hands are also covered by bugs, not the meat larva, but silkworms. I'm not afraid, I even enjoy what I'm seeing, I used to do this when I was a child, grab them by the handful at the farm, then I went scaring other kids and laughing. Like right now, laughing. I realize I'm not playing, that I'm not running the fields in Mandaguaçu anymore. That these worms are coming out of me, of the muscles of my hand. I bring my hands to my eyes and see their little mouths, where silk threads come out. Only now their threads are bright red. They're weaving red thread with my blood. I realize I'm dying too. The only difference between me and the strawberry or the meat is who'll eat me, who lives on my death. I need to stop the worms, leave this place. I look around to spot the exit and notice the fish section isn't where it was anymore. I remember what I heard on TV once, that we can know we're dreaming when we look around and suddenly, out of nowhere, the landscape changes. I need to wake up, where's my Chickadee?

I open my eyes and see Cora on my lap. Ednardo is still driving. I watch my hands, whole. Thank God, I say, and touch my Lady over the plastic. Is everything O.K.? he asks. I say I'm fine, it was just a bad dream. It's because of stuff like that that I don't sleep, he says, sometimes dreams are even worse than real life. And the worse it gets here, the scarier it gets there. I look at him. The sun is rising. I can see the line of the road, and Ednardo in another light, without the cover of night. His eyes are sunken, looks like he's been punched twice. How long have you been up? I ask. Three days. How long? He repeats and laughs a dark laugh. Is this a dream? That I kidnapped Cora and then got a ride with a man who doesn't sleep is only the beginning and the end of the nightmare. Soon I'll wake up and be happy again, taking the bus to work, reading Nora's book on the way, wearing my uniform. I look at the rearview mirror and see a tent on the edge of the road. I look at the road ahead, then again at the mirror and see the same tent again, only farther away.

32

Cacá gives me his hand. Come on, let's eat something. I follow him to the kitchen. Cacá makes two sandwiches that look nothing like something he'd make, cheese and ham thrown between two slices of bread, without the usual mayo. I look at the time on the microwave, almost three in the morning. I think it's a good idea to eat something, but I can't, I tell him I'll save mine for later. Cacá has the opposite reaction and eats with a great appetite, with an anxiety that makes him devour the whole thing in four bites. As he swallows the last one, his phone rings. He answers. By his serious tone, by the way he straightens up his posture, I already know it's the cops. I also know it's not good news, because there's no relief on his face. Rather the opposite, the wrinkle on his brow deepens, his gaze drops to the ground. I ask if Cora is dead, it's what the primitive motherly instinct in me needs to know. I'd like to believe that for anything else a solution can be found. He shakes his head, and gestures for me to wait. He asks the person on the phone what our options are moving forward. Then he hangs up and explains the evidence suggests it wasn't an accident or kidnapping. In the absence of any messages or contact, the probability of disappearance gets higher. I take a moment to think about this word. About how vague it is, a train of hollow syllables, a simulacrum of itself. What does that mean? I ask, no longer thinking about the doors and windows of an infinite maze, but about the concrete shape of our situation. He says he doesn't know, the police don't know. Disappearance must mean this, when no one knows anything. And when are they going to solve it? I ask, already guessing the answer, which comes to me in the form of a shrug.

I get up. I walk to the living room, start rummaging through my bag. Nothing like a tragedy to turn years of effort into smoke. In less than two hours I've taken up smoking again. Heavily. I open the window, light a cigarette. The nicotine helps me think clearly. I turn to Cacá.

You know what's weird?

What?

The two of them disappeared together.

Why is that weird?

Children are usually the ones that disappear. And they vanish alone.

Not just kids. Sometimes adults too. Anything can happen. This week I saw a sign for a missing cockatiel.

Fuck the cockatiel.

Cora is a cockatiel, she doesn't know our address, she wouldn't know where to come back to.

Good thing she's with Maju then. On the other hand, why would someone take a woman with a child?

The question lingers in me. I try to imagine mild scenes, maybe practical, but nothing comes to mind. Only the usual tragedies. Cacá must also be thinking of unspeakable scenarios, because he stays still, looking at me. He starts talking again a few minutes later.

They haven't been able to reach Maju's husband.

Do you think he knows what happened?

No, he'll be in bad shape when they tell him.

I don't say anything to Cacá. I know it isn't nice of me, but I'm not one bit worried about Maju's husband. There are men out there who'd pay to have their wives disappear. Who's to say he's not one of them? And to be honest, I'm not even worried about Maju, I only care about her as far as she's involved with Cora's disappearance.

Cacá takes off his shoes, starts to pace around the room barefoot. Suddenly, I am startled. I hear him whisper our daughter's name. His eyes are closed. Talk to daddy, where are you? It's strange to see him like this. I feel like he's going off the rails, but I don't blame him, I'm not entirely sane either. I go to the sideboard, where we keep our alcohol. I shouldn't mix Klonopin with alcohol, but this sedative isn't doing anything, and I'd be lucky if this knocks me out. I open a bottle of gin and make a drink. A fancy way of saying I don't actually prepare anything, just pour the gin straight in a glass. Mixology is a luxury for those living above the disaster line—which is why you never see a factory worker or a soldier swirling or drinking from a stemmed glass, casually placing an orange twist on the rim. I was living above the disaster line. Until now, I think. I take a generous swig of my gin.

When I turn around, Cacá is sitting down, holding a tarot deck. He doesn't see me look at him, he's focused on shuffling the cards. He lays them out side by side on the coffee table. What are you doing? I ask, annoyed. He puts his finger over his lips, asking me to keep quiet. That annoys me even more.

Stop it, Cacá. You won't find anything with this crap.

Don't talk like that about my oracle.

This can't even solve eight-ball questions, let alone a disappearance.

Quiet, I'm drawing a card.

He grabs one very slowly, like the card is being pulled to the table by a magnet and it takes strength to get it out. The gesture reminds me of the time when Cacá decided to study tarot. Another one of his phases that led nowhere. He thought he might get rich as a holistic therapist in a sick neighborhood, in a sick city, in a sick world. At the time it didn't bother me, I thought it made sense, but not now, just looking at the deck makes me want to hit my husband. He finally flips the card.

The chariot, he says triumphantly, showing me the image. I told you the tarot could help.

What does that mean?

The chariot suggests initiative, achievement. But we don't even need the interpretation, the answer is in the image. Why didn't we think of it before?

I stare at him, confused.

The car. The taxi! They don't go anywhere on foot. From our building straight to the club, from the club to school, from school back to our building. And all those places are safe, in a safe neighborhood. That is . . .

Do you really think the deck knows what happened?

It can't know anything, but it can suggest things so our unconscious will find the answer. That's the principle behind the art of divination, that it projects probabilities based on what we already know, even if unconsciously. Remember what the chief said, that the solution is often inside us?

He grabs his phone, calls the police station. He asks if they've checked with other taxi stands near the club and the school. Then he hangs up and tells me they haven't done it yet but they will, for sure they'll find something. I drink the last sip. I move closer to Cacá.

I agree with you. It's very likely this situation involves a taxi driver, but do you think he'd have told the other drivers what he was planning to do?

If you look at it that way, there's no point investigating anything.

He's right, but I can't help being pessimistic. Or realistic. I share my theory with him. They must have gone to a taxi stand and, not finding their usual driver, hailed a cab off the street. After that, something we don't yet know must have happened.

I was thinking that too, he says, flipping other cards, now quickly. Then he looks at me. I told you to hire a driver.

Do you know how much a chauffeur costs?

He doesn't say anything.

Of course you don't, you've never earned a cent in this house.

I raised our daughter. You don't think that's enough?

There are tons of people who raise kids, do laundry, have a job, and even find the time to sell Avon on the side.

And you do that?

I could come up with an answer, but think it's best to stay quiet, I don't want to stir up more trouble. I decide to make myself another drink that isn't really a drink. I grab the bottle and only then notice it's nearly empty. How could you leave me at a time like this? I pour what's left in my glass. I drink. It's not enough. I think of drinking one of the liqueurs, but I'm afraid I'll end up drunk like my mother. Maybe wine is the best option: it'll numb my pain, or try to, with a lower concentration of alcohol and with Bacchus's blessing, that hedonist who for sure had a better life than me. I open the sideboard, and stare at the bottles while my mind wanders, to the illusion that life follows a trajectory, that everything will be fine in the end. That we can take the reins of our lives to get more quickly to the grand finale. Until one day I realize that I can't control anything. Worse, that there isn't even a trajectory to follow. I think I say something along these lines out loud, because Cacá looks at me. I get back to what I was doing. I grab a cabernet we'd been saving for a special occasion. I show him the bottle: isn't today a special day? He shakes his head with sadness. He realizes I'm drunk, but doesn't judge me, I've always liked that about him, that he doesn't judge or try to control anyone. I put the cabernet on the coffee table, I'm about to stick in the corkscrew but he grabs my hand, makes me turn around and look at him. Do you know what Cora asked me yesterday? I listen eagerly. Dad, what are the primate colors? We laugh. His eyes water. Mine too. I take a deep breath, exhale through my mouth. Cacá goes back to pacing around the room. He opens his arms and says:

If we never see Cora again, at least we know we gave her plenty of love. That we had fun.

Fun my ass.

He looks at me.

Do you know how many times I arrived home when Cora was already asleep? And do you know where I took our daughter the only time I took a day off work to be with her?

Where?

The Renault dealership. You had fun with her. I passed by her like a cumulonimbus.

Stop it, you're her mother.

I only gave birth to Cora. To be a mother, you need to adopt the child after birth. You're her mother. So is Maju. The two of you took care of her.

You couldn't do it because you had to work.

You wish I was working. I was fucking. I mean, fucking and working.

Cacá is surprised by what I said. Me too. I go to my purse, grab another cigarette. I light the wrong end. I get another one. I don't know why I told Cacá, but now it's done, maybe I need to let it all out otherwise I'll go crazy. I take a long drag. I look up. I didn't even know I believed in God. I point the cigarette to the ceiling, giving fire to our creator: if Cora's disappearance was a moralist lesson, please know it didn't work. I don't regret anything I've done, you hear me? I don't regret it, I say even louder, now looking at Cacá and beating my chest so hard my skin burns.

Calm down, you don't have to feel guilty.

You say that because it wasn't you.

Every married person has their stories.

My cigarette stops in the air, before it reaches my mouth. What do you mean, has their stories? Do you have a lover?

No, I never got involved with anyone, he says. And seeing I won't back off: I only went out with a mom from the neighborhood once.

I don't know what angers me more: that I was financing his lifestyle while he was out fucking during school hours or that he is telling me. Why is it that even in his treacherous slip-ups, this bastard has to be my friend? I assume he'll want to blame me, ask questions, but he doesn't say a word. Don't you want to know anything? Why would I want the details, Fer, to hurt myself? I go very close to him. Do you know how annoying it is to live with someone so understanding you can't even hate them once in a while? He coughs with the smoke. I put out my cigarette. Not for his lungs, but because I'm down to the butt. While I crush the filter on a saucer, I think that maybe Cacá isn't that nice. That maybe he confessed his sins to get revenge on mine. That he didn't want details to show me his indifference to what I do or don't do. Or maybe he just doesn't give a shit. I don't know and don't want to know. To hell with all these voices in my head, I scream so loud I must wake the neighbors. Fuck my affairs. Your affairs. Everybody's affairs. I want to know where my daughter is. There was only one kid!

What are you talking about?

The kid. There was only one. Why did no one warn me?

Now I'm the one pacing around the room, looking for answers everywhere, on the walls, anywhere.

I mean, someone did warn me. The ayahuasca warned me.

You took ayahuasca?

You think you're the only spiritual person around here? I did, Cacá. And you know what the plant told me?

Tell me.

To open the door. The plant entered my body in the middle of the Amazon forest to tell me this. Hello, Fernanda, I got a message for you, a memo, please open the door. I take a breath and continue: I saw our daughter in front of a closed door.

Can you describe this door? Cacá asks, already grabbing his cell phone.

It's a metaphor. I saw a huge Cora in front of a tiny door, about half her size. She tried the knob, but it was locked. She turned it again, got down, looked through the keyhole, and nothing. She couldn't go in.

Cacá gestures for me to continue, but I pause, impressed with the clarity of my memory. It feels like it really happened. The wooden door, the golden knob, our daughter's body too big to go in. I pace around with the cabernet in one hand and the corkscrew in the other, drinking from the bottle, in search of relief I don't know I can find.

And no one opened the door?

No, I say, still pacing, still looking for answers. Why did I never open the door for her? Why didn't I do anything with this warning from the ayahuasca? What was I thinking? I yell at him or at me or I don't even know at who, while I stare at the canvas in front of me. That sterile bathroom, with those sterile tiles, with that sterile blood. I feel so much anger it doesn't fit into my body. I raise the corkscrew. Stop, I hear Cacá yell, but I'm already slashing the canvas.

33

Finally, the city. Ednardo announces it's São Paulo, but no need to say it. I can tell this hell anywhere. All the gray buildings. Cocoons on top of cocoons, millions of cocoons. Inside it, a worm, weaving all day, all week, all life. Most will never even become moths. I at least tried to take flight, but maybe one born to weave can't wear the silk, she wears polyester and viscose, like the white army. I imagine what my maid friends are doing now, inside their tiny cocoons, turning off their alarms, washing their faces, brushing their teeth, putting their hair up in a bun, putting their uniform to go into the big cocoon to make breakfast, set the table, change diapers, feed babies, arrange toys. Which is good, because with so much to do, they won't be at the square before seven.

I fix my hair in the rearview mirror, I don't want to arrive a mess. I'm patting down my hair when I notice something strange. We were driving up the interstate, but now Ednardo exits. I look away from the mirror, look in front and see we're driving into a poor neighborhood. Neighborhood is a compliment, it's a handful of unfinished cocoons. I assume Ednardo is taking a shortcut to get to the other side of the highway, to take a U-turn, but no, he goes on. What are we doing in this dump? I think. A moment later, like he can hear me, he looks at me. I have a quick pitstop. I say: O.K., though there's nothing O.K. about this. I want to ask what kind of stop, but he's more quiet by the minute. Maybe this is a drug run. Maybe this is the quick stop, a quick business transaction, a purchase, I think, and suddenly things fall into place. It must be for all the weed or crack that this man doesn't sleep. That he can't stop tapping the wheel. That's why he was in jail, not smuggling.

I look for the dealer's house, what's a crackhouse like? Can I wait in the truck or must I get off? And what if they shoot? A police raid, and I go to jail for no reason, and they find Cora later in an absurd circumstance? The authorities asking if it's stolen jewels in my bag.

The truck drives by the full cocoons, who knows how many worms are in one. Some of them are early risers, with their heads sticking out. Suddenly, a woman living alone in the Tokyo Suite seems like a privilege. I was rich and didn't know it. Now I don't have anything anymore, and not having anything, I still have a lot to lose. I start praying the Our Father. Ednardo turns to a bigger street, a little market on one side, a check cashing spot on the other. He drives a bit more, I hear him press the gas pedal—when we're tired we're so sensitive to any sound, so I even hear the silence next, then the motor until it stops at a corner, at a gas station. Thank God, a gas station. I relax, but not too, why put gas here, in the middle of nowhere?

There must be a reason, because Ednardo knows the worker there, calls him by his name. He asks to fill up the tank, pays with a credit card. Then he tells the man: I'm going inside. The man nods. I look around. The gas station is small, there's a tiny convenience store and a bathroom, he can only be talking about the bathroom. Ednardo starts to look for something behind his seat, I imagine he's looking for a roll of toilet paper, why didn't he offer it to me when I needed it? He's still looking and I want to suggest he can ask the man out there for a newspaper, he'll get newspaper stuck on his behind, but that's still better than the alternative. But then he pulls out a big bag. Not a backpack or a plastic bag, but a sack, maybe made of nylon, a string tying it up. He puts the sack under his arm. I'll be right back. Honk if you need anything.

He slams the door. I stay there, watching him walk away. He walks past the other pump, past the dump that's the convenience store, toward a door I hadn't noticed, an office or storage room or somebody's house. He knocks, gets the sack from under one arm and holds it with both hands. Maybe he's the dealer, bringing a shipment from Bolivia, Paraguay, that country next to Paraguay. I can't tell if someone opens the door or if he opens it himself, I can't see from here. He looks inside, goes in. The worker who was at the pump now goes to the tiny house and sits on a chair by the door. I can picture Ednardo doing his business, putting the sack on the table, weighing the merchandise, getting the money. Or maybe I'm crazy and the man isn't doing anything. But Jesus Christ, what is he doing? Whatever it is, it's not my problem anymore. I'm in São Paulo, I can take a cab, but looking at the rearview mirror I don't see any. I see a car, a grocery cart, a truck, but no white vehicles. Poor only take a taxi when they're dying. And just thinking of getting into another car, with another driver, I'm nervous again. Maybe Ednardo is a dealer, an addict, but I know him. He's trustful, or at least that's what I want to believe, though it's been fifteen minutes and he hasn't come back yet.

34

I wake up with the sunrise. I look around, the ashtray overflowing, the canvas in pieces. My mouth, a stale paste of Klonopin, alcohol, and nicotine. I remember why I'm waking up to this and pain instantly lands on my chest. I go from sleep straight to panic, scouring my phone for new information. No news from the police or anyone else. I grab Cacá's phone, I know the password, Cora told me, her birthday. The school group chat is quiet, no updates from Neide or the other maids.

I get up. I need to do something, anything. I go to my daughter's room again, with the childish hope I'll see her or find some clue my tired eyes missed the day before. Without thinking, I open her closet, look at her clothes. On the pile of t-shirts, there's one balled up. Cora must have put it there herself. I'd asked Maju to teach her how to fold her clothes. I grab it and bring it to my face. I smell the fabric, and inhaling brings my daughter back for a second. At first it feels good, her cologne and fabric softener, but suddenly that same smell makes me nauseous. It must be the wine, the gin, the bottles from last night. I go to the bathroom, kneel down in front of the toilet, but the vomit doesn't come. I go to the balcony to get some fresh air. It makes no difference. I need more, the entire atmosphere.

I get my phone, put on my flip flops. I see myself enter the elevator. I turn my back to the mirror, so I won't register my reality quite yet. I walk past the lobby, Chico is already there. I exchange a dry good morning, sly. He knows what's happening and doesn't have the courage to face my despair. I walk out to the sidewalk, breathing, remembering my daughter's obsession with only steeping on the black tiles, or was it the white ones? Something I found unusual to the point I told my therapist, who said that was common with children, and sometimes with adults.

Do me and my daughter look alike? I could never tell. Cora has always been one of those kids who doesn't look much like either parent. Mom, I say out loud. I repeat loudly, almost screaming, while I walk into the empty square, only the trees as my witness. One of them is huge, full of roots. I'm angry at its stability. It's easy to be a plant and have no memory. It's easy to be a plant and have no will. In its place, I'd also never fall. The way I fall now, on a bench, without even bothering to clean the pigeon shit stamping my butt.

I think about Yara. The truth is that I never stopped thinking about her, even while all this is happening she hasn't left my mind, she only went out of focus, like a blurry background to my drama. It's too early to call her, the day has barely started, but fuck it. I call her, it rings four, five times. She answers, with the voice of someone who was sleeping. Is everything O.K.? Have you found Cora? I say we haven't. I start to cry. Fat, silent tears that roll down my neck, the kind people shed when they hear of someone else's tragedy, a layer of styrofoam to pad their discomfort. I feel the tears reach my collarbone, maybe they'll puddle there like water after the rain. The crying offers some relief, a kind of peace, and I'm feeling almost ready to talk again. Without having planned it, I say: if we don't find Cora, I'll leave everything to be with you. And as if that weren't enough, I continue: forever. She doesn't say anything. The silence stretches out and I wonder if we got cut off. Yara? Sorry, she finally says. I haven't answered because I'm still half asleep. Then after another pause: but of course, we'll be together. Now I'm the one who doesn't say anything. And I couldn't anyway, my crying has turned into blubbering. She notices. She's going to say something, but I don't have the stomach to swallow another piece of styrofoam. I say I have to go and hang up.

I get up, take off my flip flops. I walk barefoot on the earth, the sharp pebbles hurt the bottom of my feet and I like it, I go on stepping on them. With all this pain, my body ache is almost a relief.

35

I don't know how but I feel he's coming back. I get my eyes off Cora and know what there is, Ednardo walking toward us. It's like watching a movie, the leading man coming out of a mysterious place and getting into a truck. I think I'm going crazy from exhaustion, it isn't possible, because the image still looks like the movies, he looks like an actor, an unfamiliar air, and I don't know why. He carries the same bag, which looks full, maybe as full as before. His clothes are also the same, but there's something else . . . He opens the door, gets in as if nothing, throws the bag in the back. Everything O.K. here? I say yes and then I smell it. Bozzano, the same after-shave Lauro used. That's why he looks different, he shaved, washed his hair, now I see up close that it's wet, combed different. I laugh, laugh at my silly, my crazy, my scares, the necklaces and rings I'll throw on the cops' table, saying: look, it's plastic jewelry, I only got a ride with this dealer. I laugh so much my shoulders shake, Ednardo staring at me. What is it? Nothing, I say, and try to hold it in. He'll be offended if I tell him what I thought. I think if this was before, he'll insist a bit more, ask again why I laugh, maybe tell me about some aunt or cousin who laughed for no reason and how hard it is for him to let go and laugh like this, but he's too tired, he's like a doormat in front of a house full of kids, not even a shave can make him more than a shell of a person right now.

We drive into the city. I feel relief and a knot in my chest at the same time as I see the streets, the same the bus takes, the

Muay Thai gym, the candy store. With each building, my chest is more knot. I want to cry, but I also feel like I've been washed with baby powder. The tears won't come out. Only my nose drips, like two eyes out of place. I look at Ednardo. And when we're the ones at the wheel and it still doesn't make sense? He thinks for a moment. It never makes sense, he says. Then he gives me a handkerchief. A cloth handkerchief, I hadn't seen one in years. With squares, light blue and white, his name sewn in navy thread. I wonder who did that, who took time to pick the thread that matched the fabric, who sew all those lines on the first letter. I let the person who hugged Ednardo with this handkerchief hug me too, as I hug Cora. How much longer?

Not much, about five minutes. It's time to think about the practical stuff. I need to have everything ready when we get there. I fold the handkerchief careful, put it on the dashboard. I ask Ednardo if I can pay him. He says, no, of course not. He must pay me for the company, he talked my ear off, he doesn't even know how I stand it. I'm grateful for him, grateful in the way we can only feel for someone we won't see again. When we get the check and no one can ruin the ending anymore. Normally I won't give him anything, I've always been stingy, or careful with money, as Lauro liked to say, but now having money doesn't matter to me anymore. Maybe Ednardo will make good use of it, maybe he'll buy the pills he likes so much. I put my fingers in my bra, grab two bills, and put them discreetly under the handkerchief. I was going to wake up Cora, but I change my mind. I'm afraid she'll ask for her mom in front of him. I just get my things, check I'm not forgetting. I didn't even see your daughter awake. I told you, children only wake up in the middle of the night when they're sick. He shakes his head, like sleeping is an act of rude. Then he looks at Cora again. What's her name? I think for a moment and say: Ana. Pretty name, he says. I remember she chose it and smile.

Then I ask him to turn around. I want him to stop on the

other side of the taxi stand. The square is big, some people even call it a park. It takes us a few minutes to go around it. Here is O.K., I say. He parks. He asks if I need help getting out. I say no, I already put my Lady into my purse, my purse under my arm, the arm under Cora. With my free hand I hold the grab handle. I think I'm really not a skank, getting off all clumsy like this. When I'm on solid ground, I say: go in peace, and wave at him. He waves back. The truck leaves. I look around, worried someone will see me. The only person on the street is a man with a dog, one of those you can never tell if he's up early or hasn't even gone to bed. Still, I let my hair down. Everyone has only seen me with my hair up in a bun, with my white uniform. The few times I wore something else, some people didn't even know me. They can't connect the maid to the person. They must think our boss deflates us like a balloon and puts us in a cupboard after our shift is over. But I don't want to be seen at all. I quickly go to the square, then to a corner where no one will see us, behind a few big trees that are all roots. I know this bench because I come here to read sometimes. Now it looks even more hid, sunlight can barely get through the leaves, it's always dark under this fig tree. Which is good, because I don't want to scare Cora. I wake her up gently, blowing on her little face. She opens her eyes slow. Where are we? Almost home, I say. Then I explain we're going to do something real cool. A game, a dare. She loves that stuff, gets all excited when her friends say they dare her to do something. I explain she'll have to get home alone, like a big girl. Maju will hide behind this fence at the park, watching you. Cora will leave the park, cross the street when Maju says, go to the building, then ring the intercom. If you can't reach it, you must call Chico. You only win the game if you get into the building, O.K.? She says O.K. And you can't tell anyone where Maju is. It's a secret, like hide and seek.

Then, I start to get my Chickadee ready. Or to get me ready, she's already prepared. I fix her hair with all my love, then put her hand on her sheep. Before she goes, I hold her shoulders. Maju will never forget you. Now you go. I'll watch you, O.K.? She walks kind of funny, like she has a limp. Maybe because she's wearing only one shoe. I go closer to the fences by the street. As soon as she leaves the square, I yell her name. I say she can cross. Quick, quick. She obeys. Soon she's on the other side. She starts to walk but then stops. I get nervous, what's she doing? Soon I realize she only steps on the white tiles. Good thing she's quick, in a second she's by the entry. She gets on her tiptoes and presses the button. She also calls for the doorman. As soon as Chico comes out, I dry my face and turn away.

ACKNOWLEDGEMENTS

To Anauila Madalosso, Clara Giacon, the Yawanawá community, Eva Madalosso Patalano, Filó, Gustavo Rocha and his Happy Cocoon, João Bosco, José Ferreira dos Santos, Krishna Mahon, Lucinei Gomes de Araújo, Mara Alves de Souza, Nilson and Sônia Magalhães, and Regina Gomes da Silva for the lessons.

To Dedé Bevilaqua, Mateus Baldi, and Natalia Timerman for their readings.

To Ana Paula Hisayama, André Conti, and Lúcia Riff for everything.

And to Pedro Guerra, my partner, for everything and more.

About the Author

Giovana Madalosso is a Brazilian writer and screenwriter. She has been a finalist for the Biblioteca Nacional Award and the São Paulo Prize of Literature. *The Tokyo Suite* is her English-language debut.